CW00850660

THE SAILOR'S LOST DAUGHTERS

Emma Hardwick

COPYRIGHT

Title: The Sailor's Lost Daughters

First published in 2020

ISBN: 9798631799677

BOOK CARD

Other books by Emma Hardwick

The Urchin of Walton Hall

Forging the Shilling Girl

The Scullery Maid's Salvation

The Widow of the Valley

The Christmas Songbird

The Slum Lady

The Vicar's Wife

The Lost Girl's Beacon of Hope

CONTENTS

1

THE DEMISE OF ARTHUR EDWARDS

"Right then, I'm off!" announced a cheerful Arthur Edwards, putting on his hat and coat by the front door. As a foundry foreman, he'd have a hard night ahead of him ordering the lazy and feckless amongst his men to keep working. He would be glad to be back after yelling through another nightshift.

Home for the Edwards' was Angel Meadow. The family were lucky to be able to afford three rooms to live in, instead of one, unlike most of the other impoverished tenement residents of Manchester's most notorious slum. With some modest savings, enough to get by for a couple of months, they were fortunate enough not to live hand to mouth. It was that small cushion of cash that kept them from sinking any lower, should an unforeseen problem creep up on them. They always tried to add in a shilling or two when they could to the kitty. For the less prosperous ones running out of money meant the workhouse.

Sat by the kitchen window was Elsie, their seamstress mother, busily repairing a basket full of clothes before the light of the day faded. Set upon a small table was her sewing machine, with a wicker basket at either side and a simple wooden work stool in between.

It would be in those simple lodgings that Agnes was born in 1848, and two years later, Grace. Their parents were kind souls, and the two little girls grew up happy, despite the hardship. From a young age, Agnes was realistic and knew the family clutched at the lowest rung of society's ladder. Grace would always view her existence through a child's eyes. She didn't see the cracks and flaws. She was blinkered, cossetted in the warmth and security provided by their parents.

Above the kitchen were a couple of bedrooms. Arthur and Elsie slept in one, the girls the other. The privy out in the courtyard was shared with ten other families in the tenement block. It was the only real discomfort that Grace consciously remembered suffering in her youth. Those freezing winter's nights, walking to decant the contents of an unexpectedly full chamber pot into the midden by the privy. Tiptoeing over the sodden ground, reeking of pestilence was dreadful.

Although they had humble accommodation, Elsie kept it clean. That in itself felt like a fulltime job. It was a paradise compared to some other dwellings in the area.

There was a constant battle against rats and cock-roaches, and the soot from the great chimneys produced a continual cloud of black dust that settled upon everything. In winter, heating the kitchen was a challenge despite the stove blazing for most of the day. The hot plate had another important purpose. Elsie was determined to iron every piece of clothing that she washed so she could kill the mites that had made homes within it.

She was a good housekeeper, disciplined with rationing their meagre supply of food, and she ensured a good meal most nights. It usually consisted of broth with potato, cabbage or carrot. A small piece of meat was an occasional luxury once or twice a week. She would save the stock from the meat and bones she cooked on a Sunday, and use it to flavour the soups for the rest of the week. It always surprised innocent little Grace that her mother could turn so few ingredients into such a feast.

Neither parent was a drinker which was a rarity for the area. Drunkenness tended to provide their neighbours with a welcome escape from the grind. Arthur and Elsie had joined the Manchester and Salford Temperance Society at the height of its popularity in the 1840s, finding it a blessing. It provided a meeting place and an opportunity to learn to read and write. Arthur proved himself to be a diligent and reliable man, and that had secured his promotion to foreman at the foundry. For them, a tea or coffee at home was sufficient. Not supporting the local boozer every night improved their modest financial lot. They wasted not a penny.

Arthur had a knack for storytelling, a cheap and rewarding form of family entertainment. The children would sit with their father by the fireside at night, listening to his fairy tales about dragons, princes and faraway lands. The vivid adventures enthralled his children, Grace in particular. It allowed them to access a world they would never experience in reality. The narratives that Arthur conjured up in his mind every night saved the family from the drudgery they all experienced throughout the day.

Being a seamstress, Elsie neatly patched the girls' clothes and sometimes made them new ones if they could be eked out from the offcuts. Beautiful quilts made out of small snippets of cloth and lace covered their narrow bed. The two happy children thought they were very fortunate to have such a beautiful home.

The only thing Arthur and Elsie ever fought about was schooling.

Arthur believed they needed a formal education which was highly unlikely in Angel Meadow's Charter Street Ragged School. It shared the building with a dancing saloon of the lowest class. With its gaudy decorations, it was a magnet for thieves and prostitutes who frequently met there. The school governors were attempting to buy the building and force the dancing saloon to find another venue, until then, it would fall desperately short of the required standard.

Elsie thought the girls needed a trade.

"Arthur, I have made a living as a seamstress, and I can pass those skills on. What good will it do Agnes and Grace if they go to school, but have no trade? Knowledge alone does not pay the bills, Arthur. And, unlike you, there are few opportunities for them to aspire to in the workplace," berated Elsie before snapping, "you live in another world!"

"Elsie, there is more to life than working. You see how their minds come alive with the stories. They are curious and love to learn. Perhaps we should think further than merely teaching them to survive in this godforsaken place? You can be so blinkered at times!"

Since the two parents had spent a considerable amount of time educating themselves at the temperance hall, a compromise was made. In the evenings and on Sundays, the girls were to work on their reading, writing and do arithmetic. In the mornings, when Arthur was sleeping after his shift, Elsie would keep an eye on them as they learned to sew.

At first, Agnes and Grace led very sheltered lives. Going to the ragged school was an experience they were not prepared for. Every morning, Elsie would wake them and dress them for school. She did her best to ensure that they were warm and always packed something for them to eat. The usual piece of dry bread and cube of cheese was carefully put into two oilskin bags, one for each girl.

The benefit of learning at home was that there was less exposure to the misery of the streets beyond. St Michael's Flags was two streets from their house, an ugly lump of a church surrounded by a graveyard that was paved over. The slabs were repeatedly stolen. There were patches where the corners of coffins protruded out of the bare earth. On cold winter nights, their neighbourhood friends would sit under the warm quilts and tell stories of restless spirits roaming the streets because their graves were disturbed.

The loving parents managed to shield their children from the shame of poverty, but they were ill-equipped to shield them from the brutality of it.

There were two distinct classes of folk living in this overcrowded hell hole. There were old established responsible families, like the Edwards' who were regarded as the salt of the earth. Then there was the influx of drunken settlers of the industrial revolution, expecting to swap agriculture for lucrative manufacturing work in the big city of Manchester. They would be left brawling, scuffling, fighting, and drinking, indulging in many a depraved pastime in the grinding poverty of the slum. It had been happening since the turn of the century.

After the invasion of starving Irish during the Great Famine in the 1840s, the locals didn't believe that Angel Meadow could get any worse, but it did. It spiralled entirely out of control until it descended into a pit of horror that would torture its weary inmates for many more decades. Reporters said in hot summers, housing inspectors found men, women and children sleeping naked in double beds, such depravity they had never seen. In other houses, the poor lay on the floor, on mattresses made of wood shavings piled beneath old blankets. For the poorest, everything was pawned and sold until there was nothing left. In the worst houses, the windows were sealed shut, and the ceilings were so low that only the youngest could stand upright. The privies were overflowing, and the passages leading to them were full of faeces. It was the perfect breeding ground for disease.

But, it wouldn't be illness or disease that killed Arthur, it was his wage packet. Arthur was always the laughing stock of the late shift because he didn't join them after work for a toot at the pub.

One Friday, he had collected his week's earnings from the wage office at the end of his evening shift. Usually, he would go straight home after a short stop at the foundry's tuck shop to buy a few sweet treats for the family. But this Friday was different. He had the chance of some extra hours which he took. *The extra money is always welcome.* At just gone one in the morning, his long day finally ended.

Arthur and a couple of brothers Billy and Robert Needham walked back towards their homes. The less sensible lads trundled off to fritter away their extra earnings betting on some rat baiting at the Dog and Duck.

Keen to get home, Arthur had suggested they take a shortcut down one of the narrow ginnels. Suddenly, there was a rhythmic clank of clogs against the cobbles. A gang of scuttlers ambushed them.

There had been talk of the extra work at the foundry. An insider at the wages office had tipped the gang off when their quarry would be wending their way home. As the workers entered a dark alley, they saw the glint of a blade and heard the metallic jangle of thick belt buckles—removed to become brutal lashing weapons.

The smell of stale, boozy breath was thick in the air. The Meadow Lads were a fiercely territorial and organised gang. Vicious fighting broke out between rival groups on an almost daily basis. Even though the skirmishes often resulted in gruesome injuries and sometimes death, the police and courts proved ineffective in stemming the rising tide of violence.

One lad grabbed Arthur and demanded his wages, another grabbed Robert. They handed the money over to them. *Better to get away with your life than die for money. A dead man can't support his family.*

If it had ended there, things would have worked out well—but it didn't. Billy Needham didn't hand over his pay packet. He turned and ran for his life. Angered by Billy's disobedience, a fight broke out. The scuttlers took it upon themselves to give the two men a good beating.

"Let's rough 'em up a bit! Teach 'em a lesson!" yelled Davie Gleech.

Arthur caught in the middle of the melee, lost his footing in the darkness. Helpless as he lay on the floor, the gang turned all their anger on him. Seeing a fleeting chance for escape, Robert fled too.

From the end of the alleyway, the two brothers watched the violent savages kick a defenceless Arthur as he lay on the floor. Mercilessly, their brass-tipped clogs dug into him, bludgeoning his face to a pulp. One blow was so hard it almost gouged one of his eyes clean out of the socket. Arthur began to bleed heavily from the lips, and he choked on the loosened teeth dancing about at the back of his throat.

His abdomen was on fire as the kicks landed on his soft belly. Not wanting to be identified if the man survived, Davie Gleech plunged his blade into Arthur's back. It was buried so deeply, it took Davie three attempts to pull it out, his prey's blood making the smooth wooden handle slip against his rough fingers.

> "Come on, lads, let's leave him to sleep that off,"
> laughed a triumphant Davie. "Folks around here
> will learn to fear our gang more than those feeble
> Bengals, sure as eggs is eggs, lads. They fight more
> like girls!"

Johnny Tomlinson ruffled Davie's hair as he joked:

> "Come on then, let's get you cleaned up before the
> coppers catch us. It's time to count our winnings! I
> reckon we should spend some of that good
> fortune down the pub! Must be a good few

shillings there! You can stump up a round of ale for your loyal lads, Davie?"

"We can drink for a week like lords on this, boys!" laughed their ring leader, the blood on his hands staining the two precious pay packets. "Who needs to do an honest day's work when you can earn a month's worth in five minutes?"

Johnny looked down at Arthur and kneeled beside him. He was barely conscious, his breathing a shallow gurgling rasp. Checking him over, he spotted something important. Johnny bent over, grabbed the chain and ripped Arthur's fob watch off his person. Keen to leave the scene of the crime before he was caught, Arthur's finger was broken as his wedding ring was stolen.

"Come on, Johnny, or we'll be up in front of the beak."

Down on the floor, Arthur's eyes flickered closed as he lost consciousness.

Once the coast was clear, Billy Needham and his brother were gravely disturbed to see the bloodied, unresponsive lump of a man on the dirty, cobbled floor. They were glad it was almost too dark to see. It spared them some of the horror of the vision of their friend so badly brutalised.

They picked Arthur up, and took an arm over each shoulder and made their way back to his home. His feet trailed behind them, noisily juddering along the uneven surface as they dragged him back to safety.

They knocked on the door tentatively, seeing Elsie waiting up for him, her tired face lit up by the oil lamp in the kitchen. They didn't want to disturb the girls. The shock of seeing their father in this state would be a memory they would take to their graves. Elsie looked at the clock on the mantlepiece. *Why is Arthur knocking? He must have lost his key, the silly fool. He never pays attention to important things.*

The door swung open, but rather than see an apologetic Arthur, she saw Billy and Robert Needham supporting her unconscious husband. At first, with his head lolling down, she thought he was ill, then she saw his blood-splattered clothing.

Arthur was carefully man-handled onto the kitchen table. There was no way they could get his unconscious body up the narrow spiral stairs. Elsie was bereft as she listened to the lads explaining how her husband had ended up in such a state. Her beloved Arthur was so badly injured only his clothes gave away his identity. She saw the rip marking where his grandfather's watch had been. His eyelids had swelled up so much they rose above his bruised brow and cheekbones. His split lips were fatter than his wife's slender wrists. Sensing the end was near, after much deliberation, Elsie asked Billy to fetch the girls from their slumber.

After thirty minutes of tending, this kind soul, a fellow who never did any harm to man nor beast, died on their kitchen table in the early hours of a Saturday morning.

The Needham brothers looked on, devastated by his passing. Grace and Agnes were beside themselves; they were so cossetted by their parents; they had never witnessed this level of brutality in all their years.

The usually calm and collected Elsie didn't succumb to sorrow, but to rage. Her life had just had a wrecking ball through it, all for the sake of a few shillings. Something had to be done. The powers that be let them terrorise the slums. *Well, no more!*

Elsie knew that the leader of the Meadow Lads, Davie Gleech, drank at the Weaver's Arms pub. While the throng of friends and neighbours mourned, Elsie slipped away, silently picking up a poker and a small, but very sharp, knife before she left. She slid both items under her coat and calmly walked to the Weaver's Arms.

2

THE SHOWDOWN AT
THE WEAVER'S ARMS

Nobody took any notice of Elsie as the heel of her hands thudded against the swing doors to the pub. It was badly lit, poorly ventilated and had a steep dark staircase leading to an upper room. Packed to bursting with Irish men, it was as hot as an oven. Nearest to her were men smoking short clay pipes, eating snacks of bread and cheese. Behind them were several more tables where chaps were gambling at cards or dominoes. At the very back, the entertainment that night was bar skittles and bareknuckle fighting. The Weaver's was a den for thieves, scuttlers and fallen women. On display was plenty of faded finery to show that the drinkers were on their way down not the way up. Barefooted boys got a clip around the ear for running between the tables drinking their pa's beer. The women were either touting for business, collapsed, stone drunk or working hard on worsening the next day's hangover. Candles flickered amongst the whirling tobacco smoke, and behind the haze, on the walls were a series of pictures of champion boxers.

A young man with a week-old beard and a prison haircut was entertaining them. He swung his pint from left to right as he sang bawdy Irish folk songs. Drunken men and women joined in at the choruses, slurring, wailing and clapping along.

When he finished, a lanky, pasty-looking lad, nicknamed 'Pipe Cleaner' stood on an old tea crate, his head almost hitting the ceiling. He began furiously playing a jig on a tin whistle. The singers now became dancers, jumping, cheering and tapping their feet as if they were puppets on a string. The fun was fast and furious.

Elsie didn't join in with the entertainment. She was on a mission to find Davie Gleech.

Davie and a few diehards were propping up the bar. Elsie stood in the shadows for a while, watching the party. She would have to calculate her actions well. Davie eventually slumped into a chair, laughing so hard he could no longer speak.

The gang leader was an excellent example of his sort. There were signs of manhood developing over the top of his boyish face. He had close-cropped hair with a long fringe. They all wore the uniform of a scuttler, a tight-fitting flat cap, and a handkerchief around the neck. This was finished off with a loose jacket and flared, bell-bottom trousers more typical of sailor's attire.

Pipe Cleaner began another popular jig, and more singing and dancing broke out. Many of the gang lads decided to join them, forming a circle of revellers around the tea crate. Davie was the worse for wear, having worked hard to spend the night's windfall as soon as possible. He stood up, tottering about, clapping out of time, his drunken head dazed and rolling from shoulder to shoulder. The tune was one of the most popular in Pipe Cleaner's repertoire, and more people joined the throng at his feet.

Like Moses parting the Red Sea, Elsie saw a pathway form, straight and narrow, leading directly to Davie. She seized the opportunity fate granted her. Sidling along the wall, Elsie was within arm's reach of her foe. She took the knife out of her pocket and gripped the handle tightly. With a deep breath, she unleashed her fury and plunged the blade deep into his neck artery, using every ounce of strength she had.

Davie's pals were drunk and slow, and it took them a while to comprehend what was happening. She wasn't going to need the poker. Blood from the jagged wound spurted rhythmically into the air like the water in a country house fountain. Elsie's clothes were saturated with gore. On the walls, the red spots started to combine and form streaks. It was like a scene from an abattoir. She was mesmerised by the sight, horrified, and it rooted her to the spot.

She didn't see the person who coshed her as she flew forward through the air, unable to stop herself. Landing on the ground, she cracked her head on the corner of the hearth. It was to be a fatal blow for poor Elsie.

Gleech's murder suddenly turned the Edwards' tragedy into a celebration for the others in the Meadow. The villain who had been a menace for years was dead.

The burial of Elsie and Arthur side by side at St Michael's Flags had a bittersweet sentiment. Arthur's brutal demise was avenged by his wife, Elsie, and in death, they were together. People were glad Elsie had slain one of the most savage criminals in Angel Meadow. The Meadow Lads wisely decided to leave Agnes and Grace alone. The police would call on them first if the girls were harmed.

But, the death of their parents in a short space of time left Agnes and Grace in a bind. They had never needed to fend for themselves before. Their elders always took charge. Arthur and Elsie had left them their small nest egg, but with limited experience of running a household, how long it might last was something of a mystery. If they struggled to find work, they would quickly find themselves in deep trouble.

With less income, they needed to find a smaller place to live. Angel Meadow landlords weren't too fussy who their tenants were as long as they were good payers. With a month paid upfront, thankfully, the girls found somewhere.

They moved into a tiny back-to-back. It was pitiful compared to where they had been, but they knew they could pay the rent, which was the primary consideration. The back-to-back had a room downstairs where they had a small stove to cook. The table, chairs and beds from their old house came with them. It just fitted in. They shared the bedroom upstairs and divided it in half with a curtain to offer a small amount of privacy. Together with the colourful quilts on their bed, the room was cheerful.

Agnes and Grace set about finding their mother's former customers. Within a few months, they could get by and still have some money for the occasional luxury. In fact, a lot of people thought that the Edwards girls were very grand indeed.

If Grace was beautiful, Agnes was spectacular. She was as tall as Grace and had the same blue eyes, but her straight ash-blonde hair was a little longer and fell to her waist. Her skin was as fair and as blemish-free as the porcelain in the factories. She had a high forehead and cheekbones, a straight nose and a strong jawline. Her smile, on the rare occasions she gave it, was wide and displayed two rows of perfect teeth.

Agnes had ample allure but was devoid of charisma. She had inherited her mother's no-nonsense practicality. In contrast, Grace's peaceful, dreamy nature had flourished in her like it had in her father. As they found their feet, independent-living harshly thrust upon them overnight, these characteristics served the pair well. Stoic Agnes took the responsibility of running the household. A pliable Grace simply complied with all her sister's domestic decisions and worked as hard as she could to keep her happy.

The two sister's lives ran like clockwork. They were up and dressed by seven o'clock every morning. They ate a small breakfast and then began their needlework. Agnes collected garments that needed repairs in the morning, and Grace returned the mended clothes in the afternoon. There was a hustle and bustle around their small home with other customers paying them a visit in between. They earned a reputation as good, reliable workers and business was booming. There was always tea on the stove, and the little house was warm and cheerful in the bleak environs of the slum.

In time, Agnes, ever practical and methodical got a reputation for her fast, detailed work, and soon she was sought after by a better class of client—the society dressmakers.

3

THE CHANCE MEETING

Diego Alaniz was lost. It was the third time that he had walked down Angel Street, and he could still not find the number he was looking for. He gave up hope on the fourth attempt and looked around for his cab and driver who, much to his annoyance, also proved elusive.

Manchester was his least favourite place in the world. He only agreed to visit the smog-clad city as a favour owed to his life-long friend Eduardo Garcia.

Diego had promised him that on his next trip to Manchester, he would try and locate his precious sister, Maria, and return her safely to Spain.

A few years earlier, Maria had a whirlwind romance in Barcelona with William Eaton, a man who like all seasoned heartbreakers, had promised her the world but failed to deliver. Their son Pedro promptly followed their nuptials, too quickly for Eduardo's liking, who wondered if it was a shotgun wedding. The couple started well, but it would turn into a disastrous marriage. Eaton was an English conman with a knack for turning out forged paintings by the old masters. It became clear to Eduardo that William was neither a gentleman nor a man of means. So prolific was his deceit, many collectors throughout Europe were conned into buying his bogus works. When he was sentenced at Bow Street Magistrate's Court, news of his conviction made it into the international press. All Eaton's assets were impounded to compensate those who had been swindled, and he was given a long spell in Newgate prison as punishment. Thankfully, Eduardo's wealth meant he could bring Maria home to Barcelona, providing of course, that Diego could find her. All they had to go on was the newspaper article saying he left behind a wife and son in a downbeat area of the city.

The weather in Manchester was particularly foul for spring. Black clouds hovered low in the sky and merged with the dark slate roof tiles. A bone-chilling wind was blowing off the River Irk into the maze of streets in Angel Meadow. The place was hellish and horrible, not at all heavenly as its pretty name suggested. The hunched-up people shuffling along the pavements were a reflection of the clouds, dark and brooding and burdened by the weight they carried.

Diego was aware that there was a busy market just along the way, and he wondered if he would have the good luck to find Maria there. *Someone might know of that rogue Eaton's previous address at the very least?*

Diego increased his pace as he strode down Angel Street. He noticed the cold in the air and how much his mood now matched the blackness around him. *What on earth was Maria thinking of when she eloped with an Englishman? Such a terrible, miserable, grey place.*

It was not as if Diego had never experienced living in poverty. He was simply determined that he would never live in a slum again. When his father Manuel had married his mother, Isabella, Barcelona still had some dignity. His parents had an apartment in the old Gothic Quarter, but the social decay set in with the birth of the textile industry and thousands of people swamped the area to live close to the factories. Like all the great cities of Europe, poisoned by industrialisation, it was over-crowded with Spaniards, Catalans and foreigners. It housed the wealthy in the best places and the impoverished in the slums. The city was literally bursting out of its walls. When Diego returned home lodging in doss houses with Eduardo between sailings, they ended up in Las Ramblas near the El Raval district, Spain's equivalent of the Meadow.

Diego and Eduardo chose to go to sea to escape poverty. They were fourteen years old, and the friends saw no other option for themselves. It was an opportunity to see the world, and there was a slim chance their luck would change, and they would not be trapped in a lifetime of poverty. Diego's father encouraged him, but his mother spent months praying to the Virgin and lighting candles hoping in vain for a miracle, that their son would choose another path.

The steamer they boarded was a welcome relief from the Las Ramblas slum, also ravaged by crime, disease and death. The only reason he had probably survived to this age was because of the open sea, to which he was eternally grateful.

For the two childhood friends, buccaneering had turned out to be a rewarding career choice. When they returned to Barcelona, Diego and Eduardo had just enough money to buy a rust bucket of a ship ready to be scuttled. Between them, they worked tirelessly to salvage it. Their first contract was to transport precious spices from the North African colonies along the Mediterranean coast. It proved to be a very lucrative endeavour, and from there, their profitable shipping business snowballed.

Life at sea was hard work, but it gave them freedom. Owning a business was personally and professionally satisfying. By their early thirties, they had experienced most of what the world had to offer, and their bank balances were bursting at the seams. Prosperous enough to live anywhere in the world, they never needed to work again.

Diego had experienced the pleasure of money, material goods and women of all countries of the world; but he had never fallen in love. He had never met the one woman who was more important than the sea and his wealth.

He spent a lot of time with Eduardo's family, and he was envious of the man. Eduardo had married Carmen when he was twenty-eight. She was a twenty-three-year-old Spanish beauty. Intelligent, challenging and feisty, there was no doubt that she was the matriarch who ruled her family with a rod of iron. Eduardo was the opposite. He was gentle, carefree and besotted with her.

Diego would often arrive at their villa to find Eduardo and the four boys in the garden. Playing and splashing in their crystal blue swimming pool, they pretended to be pirates on the shores of a treasure island.

"How many children are you going to have, Eduardo? There will not be enough inheritance for them all by the time you die," Diego would laugh.

"Aah, it's all Carmen's fault," he would reply with a shy smile. "She says that when she can produce a girl for me, it will be the last child. Heaven knows how she'll achieve that!"

In reality, he knew that his whirling dervish of a wife could achieve anything.

After visiting the Garcia's home, Diego would return to his own villa. The loneliness would engulf him as if he had stepped into an echoing, empty tomb. He hungered for the noise and energy that Eduardo had in his home.

Smithfield Market was a vast emporium to the south-east of the slum. It was home to thousands of merchants dealing in butter, tea, groceries, cheese, ham, spices, fish and other provisions, usually adulterated to hide their rancidity, or to stretch legitimate ingredients further. The aisles were filled with hundreds of people scratching about for the best articles they could find with the little money they had. As well as food, some stalls sold children's clothes, others adults, some overalls for the workers. There was an abundance of things to wear, but everything was patched and patched again. It was not uncommon to spot your own discarded garments, thought to be beyond repair, recycled and sported by someone else.

He passed stall upon stall, examining the owners and their passing trade. He didn't recognise anybody even vaguely similar to Maria. The vendors watched him closely, with suspicion, his exotic appearance a giveaway. A foreigner, with his olive skin and Panama hat, was an unusual sight in this area. Diego's Moorish ancestry gave him a naturally dark complexion, and often being at sea made it two shades darker. His hair was the darkest brown to match his eyes. He towered above men of average height. The heavy lifting and hauling that was the bread-and-butter work of a sailor made his body lithe and muscular. He wore a black coat long enough to reach well beneath his knees. Beneath it, his black suit was perfectly tailored and paired with a tasteful burgundy waistcoat. A cane made of ebony with a steel tip added to his sophisticated look. He had the presence of a refined gentleman, but also the absolute ruggedness of a man who had spent years at sea. All in all, it was an attractive combination.

Diego walked briskly, his head towering above the locals. He craned his neck to scan the stalls for Maria. Focused on the task at hand and not watching where he was going, he collided with someone whom he initially thought was a child. A basket went flying across the cobbles, which he chased after to atone for the impact. The clothes tumbled out of the toppled basket, getting wet and muddy from the foetid ground. He felt ashamed that his selfishness had soiled someone else's belongings.

The English rose in front of him was tall, slender and had a beautiful face. A red coat covered her from head to toe to combat the bad weather. A few of her buttons were undone, revealing a simple dress that didn't expose much of her figure. He caught a glimpse of blonde hair. Large blue eyes studied him from under her matching red hat, then she smiled broadly.

> "I am sorry, Señorita." said an apologetic Diego, handing her the basket. "Your things are all covered in mud."

> "Do not worry, Sir, I have to wash them anyway," she laughed reassuringly, trying to put the exotic gentleman at ease.

There were many women in Diego's life that he had been able to forget, but this was the reverse. Her face was beautiful, yes, but it was her smile—it radiated pure happiness and joy. The moment was now firmly imprinted on his mind, and he knew it would stay there forever. Later, whenever he came to remember it, he would feel the familiar warmth tinged with sorrow flooding his heart. For the rest of his life, this woman would be his first love. Not only physically, but spiritually and emotionally.

"I must have them laundered and return them to your stall, Señorita," he said with distinct continental charm.

"Please, it's no trouble. I promise," she laughed. "I am a seamstress, not a stallholder, they needed washing and ironing anyway."

"In that case, may I buy you a cup of tea to make up for my lack of attention?" he asked kindly.

The woman thought it over quickly and accepted in an instant.

"Follow me, Sir. I know just the place."

Grace never talked to strangers at the market, it was home to all sorts of unsavoury characters, but with this man, for some unfathomable reason, she couldn't help herself. She was like a moth to a flame.

There was a tea room on Angel Street, and she led the way. The temperance hall had set it up as an alternative to the forty-three pubs with the Meadow. Even though it was dark and dingy, there was a lively crowd within, enjoying some respite from the cold, savouring a hot sweet drink to bring some cheer to their afternoon.

"Señorita, my name is Diego Alaniz, I am pleased to meet you." He bowed with a flourish.

Grace looked on, a little stunned, yet charmed nonetheless by his flamboyant introduction.

"My name is Miss Edwards, Grace," she replied, in a much more understated fashion.

"Do you live close by?" he enquired.

"Yes, I do," she answered with a smile, hoping he didn't think less of her. "And, Mr Alaniz, since you called me 'Señorita' may I infer you are from faraway Spain?"

"Indeed, I am Miss Edwards. Do you know much about my homeland?"

"I have been very fortunate. My parents made sure my sister and I could read, and there have been many mentions of it in the newspapers and our history books."

"I was raised in a slum in Barcelona, and I too received my education from my parents. It seems we have that we have a lot in common, Miss Edwards."

He smiled, but Grace's mind had flitted elsewhere. Her face went blank as she pondered his last comment. Las Ramblas in Barcelona had a reputation throughout Europe as one of the most dangerous places to live.

3

THE SEARCH FOR MARIA EATON

Diego began to worry that he might be sullied by the reputation of the Spanish city, but he needn't have. It so happened that for Grace and Diego, their difficult and impoverished beginnings served as a catalyst. She was immediately comfortable, relieved that she didn't need to worry she was a 'mere girl from the Meadow' in this refined gentleman's presence.

Diego explained that he was looking for Maria and that her help as a Manchester local would be invaluable. Grace was keen to assist with such a worthy cause.

Every afternoon for two weeks, at four o'clock, the two friends met at the tea room as Grace returned from her deliveries. They would discuss the progress he had made with his investigation. She was drawn to the sincerity in Diego, and his earnest search for Maria and Diego was captivated by her beauty and innocence. Not that Grace was foolish or uneducated, but the world had never spoiled her, and there was no cynicism in her demeanour. Of course, she still had hope for a better existence away from the grime and crime of Manchester, but also remembered to find joy in the life she had. From their discussions, Diego had pieced together that Grace had never been in love, nobody had ever hurt her, and she was a perfect canvas on which he could paint their future.

A week into their daily encounters, Diego went to the post office, and he sent a telegraph to Eduardo in Barcelona. It read:

WILL BE HOME IN THREE WEEKS STOP FOUND HER STOP

Eduardo smiled when he received the message. He was delighted that Diego had found his beloved sister, Maria, at last.

His return message read:

THANK YOU STOP LOVE TO MARIA STOP

Diego roared with laughter when he saw the misunderstood reply. He may have found the woman he was looking for. However, he still had to find the elusive Maria Eaton. Soon his ship would have to return to Spain. There was a matter of days left to find her.

With Grace's help, it was easy to put the word out amongst the local community that Diego was looking for a Spanish woman named Maria Eaton, with a son Pedro. To bolster the chances of success in their search, Diego paid for an advertisement in the Manchester Guardian. John Coggan, the owner of the tea room, offered to accept his correspondence, for a fee of course. Every afternoon, Grace and Diego opened all the notes to see if there were any useful clues.

With the clock ticking, they were relieved to receive a note from a local hotel owner telling them that Maria was working as a chambermaid for him. The memo also advised it would 'only' cost Diego ten pounds to buy her out of her contract. He didn't care about the opportunistic wheeze. Diego would have sold his ship to buy her if he had to, such was his loyalty to his dear friend Eduardo. They were like brothers.

Diego took a carriage to the Meadow Hills Hotel, a squalid hole that catered to pedlars and sailors. He took some tea in the lounge, fearful he might catch a disease just by looking at it, never mind drinking some. Maria saw Diego before he saw her and she ran into his arms, speaking so fast that even he had problems understanding what she was saying.

"Maria, thank God that we have found you.
Eduardo has been beside himself with worry,"
said a jubilant Diego.

"¡Oh Diego! ¡Gracias a Dios que estás aquí!" cried a relieved Maria.

She continued in Spanish to keep their conversation private.

"I am going to thank the Good Virgin for bringing you here today, I'll light one hundred candles, and say one hundred Hail Marys."

She continued, getting more dramatic with each sentence she uttered. Her Mediterranean body language gave the owner some clues to the importance of the conversation. Talking louder and louder, she was now gesturing wildly with her hands.

"Let us fetch Pedro, then we are leaving. How long will it take to return to Spain?" she demanded.

Diego looked on, stunned by her manic behaviour. She kept adding to the endless list of questions that couldn't be answered, mainly because Maria wouldn't be quiet long enough to listen to Diego's responses. In the end, he gave up.

When he told Grace at their next four o'clock rendezvous that Maria was safe and staying with him at his suite in the Grand Hotel, she was surprised by how bereft she felt. *Soon, he will be gone. Forever.* She would miss him dearly. It had only been a matter of weeks in each other's company, but she had become desperately attached to him. Uncharacteristically, Grace felt remarkably jealous that he was leaving, taking Maria and her son to Barcelona, rather than her.

It dawned on Grace that in her naivety, she had allowed herself to secretly believe that there was a future for them. She thought back and noticed her imagination had pondered a myriad of romantic possibilities that had stayed firmly locked in her head—and heart. *Why didn't I at least allude to how I felt? Now, it's too late! He's leaving Manchester. And me!*

Diego had feelings of his own, but he was not prepared to share them with Grace just yet. He needed time with his mistress, the sea, to clear his head, and examine his emotions. For all intents and purposes, she was an angelic and innocent girl and he an experienced man of the world. Was this deep emotion he felt, genuine love, or just a desire to shelter her from her harsh environment? He was confused.

The situation with Maria forced his hand. His inevitable return needed to be swift. At their favourite meeting place, the little Angel Street tea shop, he would have to say a reluctant goodbye to his Gracie. He knew he wasn't looking forward to the conversation. For Grace too, it would be one of those bittersweet final moments together, with her desperate to see him one last time, yet almost too heartbroken to go.

They were in the tea room at their regular table at the back of the shop where they could see who was entering and leaving. Diego had never touched her, and she had never taken his arm while walking. Neither of them had intimated about a possible shared future, even though in their hearts, they knew they belonged together forever.

Polite small talk filled their final conversation. The communication was stilted and awkward, losing the warm natural flow it had when they were looking for Maria.

Finally, Diego broached the difficult topic neither of them wanted to contemplate.

"The trip to Barcelona is fast. Five days usually."

He looked into her eyes. Grace tried with difficulty to be cheerful and smile, but the words stung her soul.

"It is wonderful that Maria will see her family soon," she answered, appearing overly jolly and straining to remain so.

"Grace, I am sure that we will meet again when I do business here. You have shown me that perhaps I judged Manchester a little harshly. It has some beautiful redeeming qualities."

A pang of sadness overwhelmed him as he stood up to leave.

"Yes, if you ever need help again, please contact me," she said with a polite civility, still unable to share the depth of her true feelings.

"Goodbye, Grace. Thank you."

Unable to speak without betraying her emotion, her reply was a brave, but false, smile. She gave him a nod she hoped meant 'have a safe journey.'

He bade her farewell, then headed via the hotel to the railway station. There, he and Maria would travel to the Port of Liverpool for their sailing back to Spain in his cargo steamer. As he walked away, he was yearning to turn back and see Grace one last time, the words of his telegraph repeating and creating an unwelcome churning of doubt in his stomach. *Found her Stop. What if I have found 'her'? What now?*

Grace buttoned up her coat and headed back to her small back-to-back. She battled with the desire to turn and run after him. It took considerable effort to suppress, but suppress it she must.

It took Diego almost a week to sail to Barcelona. The sea was smooth for that time of the year, but there had been a stormy day when they started out, which had slowed his progress. Now it was still, he sat for hours watching the ripples, thinking. Maria prattled non-stop, and Pedro was bored, boisterous and refused to calm down. This time he didn't enjoy the noise and the energy around him. He wanted to be alone to feel his emotions. He wanted to explore the loss and the heartbreak. Somehow, instinctively, that feeling would drive him back, all the way back to the faraway shores of England and Grace.

5

THE CONFESSION TO EDUARDO

In their shared office, Diego and Eduardo sat overlooking Port Vell, Barcelona's harbour. Elegant white buildings with the blackest of wrought iron railings lined the water's edge. A mass of tall ships, steamers and fishing boats were berthed in front of them. Behind the masts was a deep orangy sunset.

"Thank you for returning Maria," said a grateful Eduardo. "Did Pedro behave on board? He's a lively little thing. He can be quite a handful at times."

"Well, he's here," chuckled Diego, "I didn't drown him!"

A smiling Eduardo was delighted to be back in the company of his closest friend once more. He had missed him.

He loved escaping the mayhem at home under the auspices of doing work with his business partner.

"Mama was so happy to see Maria that she has moved in with us. Papa is complaining because Mama is neglecting him. Carmen is complaining that I am working too late, but I am going mad there." sighed Eduardo, a little weighed down by the imposition of his new house guests.

Diego offered some words of comfort, keen to delay having to divulge something weighing on his mind. When the small talk petered out, he had no choice but to confess.

"Eduardo, I need some advice."

He shuffled in his seat, wanting to say what was troubling him, and yet not. It would mean releasing the genie of emotion from the bottle, something no man relished. Eduardo raised an eyebrow of encouragement.

Diego gave a nervous cough to clear his throat and delay his slow ease into the subject. Sheepishly, he asked:

"How do you know if you are in love with a woman?"

Relishing giving his friend his answer, Eduardo took his time to share his views. He chose to recline slowly on the long leather couch in his office, trying to conceal a smirk as he gave out a thoughtful sigh. In the meantime,

Diego did his best to hide his friendly impatience. *Tell me.*

"When she is worth more than you own. When nothing about you has value if she is not a part of it."

"Is that how you felt about Carmen?"

"Yes," Eduardo answered. "That woman is my whole world."

His friend's advice struck a chord. Diego decided to return to Manchester forthwith.

6

THE RETURN TO MANCHESTER

His mistress didn't satisfy him as she used to. Diego was restless and lonely at sea. Only Grace could fill the void he was experiencing. It was just as Eduardo said. *Nothing has any value without her.* He couldn't wait to reach dry land in Liverpool.

Diego left his fine cab and walked to the tea room where he and Grace had always met. John Coggan, serving a couple of steaming hot brews, was delighted to see him again and greeted him with a warm smile.

"Good day, Mr Diego."

"Buenos dias, John."

"Weather's a bit better out there today, Sir."

"Yes, a bit warmer, I think. The crossing was easier this time, much calmer seas."

Diego followed him towards the counter, where he discretely called the owner to one side.

"John, I need to see Miss Edwards, would you know someone who could take her a note?"

"Of course, Sir, let me just speak to my lass Kathleen. Everyone knows where the Edwards girls live. Why she can show you where to go? It's not far."

"Thank you, John," smiled Diego, "I appreciate your assistance."

The Spaniard shook John's hand and as he did so, surreptitiously pressed a folded piece of paper against his palm. He promised to thank Kathleen for her support too. Looking down, the tea shop owner was delighted to see in his hand a crisp pound note beginning to unfurl.

Kathleen was eight-years-old, going on eighty. Her local knowledge was so vast, she didn't stop speaking for a moment as she led Diego to Grace's address.

"See that street there? Sarah Adams lived down that one. She turned up out of the blue one day, eighteen and heavily pregnant. She was staying with Annie Bridges for five weeks. Annie was good to her. Gave her a bed and scraps of food. Even helped her deliver the baby. As a young mum, Sarah would never get work unless she gave up the child. She tried selling hat fancies she made at home, but it never made enough. So, one night, she walked down to the Irk and dropped the kiddy, a girl, in a blanket, into the jet-black water of the river. Sam Lloyd, Harvey and Lizzie's, son found the poor little mite floating along a minute or two later. He had to put the baby on his knee and slap her hard on the back to get her to breathe again. They've got a court case about it soon, for her trying to destroy the baby. They reckon she might be hung. Father upped and left her. She never saw him after he got her expecting."

Kathleen had a similar tale of woe down every street. It made Diego's head spin that Grace and Agnes were still living there. By the time Diego reached their destination, he felt he knew the intimate history of every nook and cranny of Angel Meadow—and every resident.

At the front door of Grace's back-to-back, Kathleen put out her hand in expectation. Diego gave her a pound note as a reward for her efforts.

"Thank you, Sir," she answered, looking down, stroking the money in joyous disbelief, unable to make eye contact with her kindly benefactor. It was a lot more than she was expecting. *I must make sure he gives me more next time!*

Diego knocked on the door. An inquisitive Kathleen was slow to leave.

"Scoot!" growled Diego. "Or I'll take my money back."

Kathleen did as she was told and skipped out of the courtyard. Moments later, a flabbergasted Grace opened the door. As she saw Diego at the threshold, she smiled with glee.

"May I come in, Señorita?"

"Oh! Of course—Señor!"

She was delighted.

2

DIEGO MAKES HIS BID

Diego thought he had better remove his hat and stoop down a fraction as he entered into the humble little home. His first impression was that it was tiny but well kept. Presuming he would want a cup of tea, Grace thought about putting the kettle on, and carefully arranged some shortbread biscuits onto an old china plate of her mother's, still in pristine condition. By the window, was her old sewing machine.

"You should have said you were coming. I so wanted you to meet Agnes, but she is not here. Tea?"

"Grace—sit down," said Diego softly, seeing that his unexpected arrival had flustered her.

She sat down opposite him at the dining table, putting down the plate between them.

"Biscuit?"

"Grace, I want to take you with me back to Barcelona."

Grace was thoughtful for a while—too long for Diego's liking—and then smiled.

"Oh Diego, I would love a job in your villa!"

"I want to take you away from this place, I want to give you a better life than you have here."

"Yes, it will be a wonderful new beginning. Your villa sounds a delight to behold. And that fresh sea air, none of this choking, thick black smog."

He took a deep breath, leant forward and gently stroked the back of her hand with his fingers. It caught her by surprise. She bit her lip, hoping he didn't notice, but he had. He looked her earnestly in the eye.

"You don't understand. I am not asking you to work for me—will you marry me, Grace?"

Grace felt like she was in a dream. The moment was surreal. She looked down at his rugged right hand, resting protectively on hers.

Ever the romantic, with her heart fit to burst with delight, Grace's mind was made up there and then.

"Yes," she answered, "yes, I will marry you!" as her eager eyes looked up and returned his gaze.

Diego stroked her hair with his left hand, then brushed his fingers forward along her blushing cheek, and slid them under her chin. He leant towards her for their first kiss.

"Grace, I'll fetch you at ten o'clock tomorrow morning, and we will go to the registry office and be married. Then we can have a few days away together? Do you need to speak to your sister?"

"Agnes won't be back from Chester for several days," she replied. "A prominent society seamstress has asked her to help her during the summer party season when she had too much work to complete by herself. The pay is good, and she is a very practical person. She will be fine."

Grace paused thoughtfully as a rare determined look formed on her face.

"Besides, I don't need to ask her, Diego, I know that I want to marry you."

He reached into his bag and took out something wrapped in brown paper, tied with string. On it was the name 'Grace'.

"A little something from my friend's wife for you", he said, as he laid the gift gently on the table. "Open it when I'm gone."

Diego kissed her again and left for his suite at the Grand Hotel, promising to collect her the next day bright and early. Using the back of one of Agnes's seamstress invoices, she wrote a brief note.

"Don't' worry about me, I am safe. Mr Alaniz and I are getting married! I shall be back soon to tell you all about it! Here are a few shillings to help with the rent."

Next, she pulled the string on the parcel, clueless about what might be inside. Her face lit up as she exposed the delicate fabric inside. Carmen had sent her a traditional black Spanish wedding dress.

Grace didn't take long to pack, she barely owned anything more than what she was stood up in.

The registry office was cold and the registrar and his assistant efficient. They had no time for love and romance, seeing countless 'loving' couples come and go, and their relationships promptly collapse.

Diego and Grace were married in fifteen minutes.

The dashing Spaniard assisted his new bride into the cab. Grace didn't know what to do or say. *Life is going to be very different from now, Gracie. No more Manchester slums.* Diego smiled at her, and the warmth of it eased her mind.

"My darling, we are going on honeymoon," he whispered in her ear.

"But Diego, I have no clothes or suitcase," she cried, "and I have sewing to do."

"I have taken care of everything," he said with a broad smile, "and Carmen, Eduardo's wife, has put together a small wardrobe for you. It's a gift from Spain. John Coggan in the tea shop says his wife can help with the needlework until Agnes returns. All that is left is for you to enjoy yourself, my dear."

He watched her face. Her expression changed from pleasant disbelief to pure joy, and he loved it.

It took the rest of the day by train and carriage to reach the Lake District cottage Diego had rented, on the picturesque shore of Windermere. Its whitewashed walls glowed in the evening moonlight. Grace thought it looked like a vision of heaven on earth. Buildings never gleamed in the Meadow. Squeezing her hand as he sensed her blissful mood, Diego purred:

"Like it? We are staying here for a month."

A shocked Grace protested:

"A month! A month! But I have so much to do back in Manchester before we start our lives together. Everything still needs attention back at home! Agnes will be furious."

"We will worry about Agnes and all those other things when we get back. Eduardo will need my help no doubt on my return too. The world won't stop turning while we are away," replied Diego softly, "but for the next month, everyone else will have to take a back seat. Now, it is only you and me."

The cottage was warmed by a large open fire. In the week before their arrival, Diego had been extremely busy making sure they had everything they would need. He had arranged for a local cook to supply meals. The furnishings were comfortable and homely. Grace suddenly felt shy, and he sensed it.

"Come to me," he beckoned, keen to put his beautiful new wife at ease.

Diego reached into his pocket and produced a sparkling three-carat ruby set in an 18-carat gold ring. Grace was stunned and delighted. *Why is this happening to me? What have I done to deserve this? That ring must have cost a fortune!* She slowly walked towards him, her eyes flitting between the ring and his face. Her smile began to broaden as her shyness melted away.

He took her hand and carefully placed the ruby ring onto her delicate finger. The excitement made Grace breathe in deeply. *Diego is so different from the men in Angel Meadow. I still can't believe my luck!* He took her into his arms and looked down to her adorable face.

"I love you, Grace. I loved you from the moment I saw you. There is something special about you that I can't resist."

He pulled her towards him slowly. His arms pressed her close to his body and held her there for a long time. Her ear resting on his chest heard his heartbeat, loud and rhythmic. Then he tilted her head up gently and kissed her.

It was their first proper embrace as man and wife. Diego felt fire surge through his body. He suppressed his passion. He dared not frighten her—his perfect blank canvas.

They climbed the small staircase to the bedroom. Diego led her towards the bed. He began exploring her slowly, and she surrendered to him. They consummated their marriage two hours later. Both were exhausted; both were satisfied.

Diego, the lifelong maritime man, didn't miss the ocean or the ship. He loved waking up with Grace in his arms. Grace never stopped talking, and Diego never stopped smiling. They would take long walks by the lakes and Grace was overawed by the beauty. It was as pretty as the lands Arthur used to describe to her, blue sky, fluffy white clouds, towering fells, glorious ancient woodland and water so clear that you could see the gleaming stones beneath your feet.

In the evenings, they would lay in bed, naked, and talk of the exciting ports they would visit as they explored the world together.

The four weeks went by too quickly. The little cottage had become their haven, and it was Grace's first taste of paradise.

At breakfast on their last day, Grace looked a little downhearted.

"I don't want to leave this place," she said quietly.

"Grace, we are married now," he laughed, "have you forgotten? We are always going to be together. That is where true bliss is."

After their meal, they packed their belongings, then looked out of their window for the cab to come and collect them. Diego kept squeezing Grace's hand protectively.

But, in the coach, as they began the journey south to Manchester, Diego had a gnawing sense of foreboding. He chose to ignore it and focused on his thoughts on his beautiful wife instead. He'd had those premonitions in his life before, and it hadn't ended well.

8

AGNES'S AWKWARD
CONVERSATION

On her return from Chester, the first thing Agnes saw was the note on the table. Her fist thumped down hard on the waxed wood as she read it. *Married? What will become of me? That selfish girl! She never thinks of the consequences of her actions! Three sheets to the wind is what she is!*

For several days, the abandoned sister was left alone, simmering about the downturn her life would inevitably take without Grace's contribution to the household. *Returning to Angel Meadow is like returning to a nightmare. The environment is terrible, but it's the people who make it worse.*

With their honeymoon over, the cab carrying Diego and Grace, clattered down the dingy cobbled streets towards the little back-to-back and Agnes. They asked the driver to go past the Angel Street tea shop, where the newly-weds gave an excited wave to John Coggan as they went past. True to form, Kathleen made sure everyone knew Mr Alaniz's business.

Agnes opened the door to her newly wedded sister, accompanied by her mysterious foreign husband.

The reception was icy cold. When Grace introduced Diego as her spouse, Agnes could have spat venom. However, by the looks of things, Diego was a wealthy gentleman. Any reservations she might have voiced about Grace's choice of partner would have fallen on deaf ears. He did have a handsome, Prince Charming look about him, and if the tables were turned, with a meal ticket out of the slum offered to her, Agnes wouldn't have refused either, she supposed. She was riddled with resentment. Diego was pleasant enough, but his sole focus was on Grace's welfare, not hers. Not only would she lose the support of her sister in the household, but she seemed to be escaping the hell of Angel Meadow, leaving her to cope on her own.

Diego and Grace knew that the note must have turned her world upside down when she read it, and they were keen to tell her that she wouldn't suffer any hardship because of their decision. They had come to discuss the future with Agnes, and they wanted her to be a part of it.

Agnes was used to men paying attention to her because of her great beauty, but Diego gave no signs of admiration at all. *How dare my little sister upstage me?* And so, she began to put a wedge between them out of pure jealousy.

"Why was I the last to know about this, Grace? Why did you not tell me on Mr Alaniz's lengthy visit earlier in the year?" she hissed sharply.

"He hadn't asked me to marry him then. He asked me when he came back all the way from Spain to find me. You were working in Chester, and I didn't have time to get a message to you. He had discussed the possibility of matrimony with his business partner in Barcelona who agreed with his idea. When he got back to Manchester, Diego wanted to marry straight away. As long as we made provision for you to run this house without me, I didn't think I needed to ask you? You are not my—father—"

"You can't just leave? How am I supposed to survive by myself?"

"I have said we—Diego— will make sure you are cared for. You will want for nothing."

Rather than being relieved that she would get some assistance, Grace was dismayed to see Agnes's face grew darker. *Money might solve some problems but not all, dear girl.*

"But aren't you happy for me, Agnes, I have met a wonderful man, and he wants to take care of me—

well, us, actually! I fail to see what the problem is? Surely you want to escape from here too?" Grace protested.

Agnes was far too angry to take an interest in whatever provision they thought they could put in place.

"What do you know about men? He is just another wealthy snake who will leave you for something better."

Grace was mortified that Agnes had insulted her husband, spouting her bile with him sitting at the same table. Diego kept his calm and attempted to retrieve the situation.

"On the contrary, Agnes," advised Diego gently. "I'll never leave or forget Grace. I have never been married before, and she is the first woman that I have wanted to be wedded to. She means the world to me. I can assure you, I have no intention of upsetting or neglecting her."

Diego had gone up a fraction in Agnes's expectations, but she was still bitterly angry about the situation. *How can Grace be so foolhardy? Racing ahead, marrying a man, a Spaniard no less, that she barely knew? She's not even seen where they will be living in Spain!*

"Miss Grace, Miss Agnes!" yelled a voice at the door, followed by a loud rapping. "Miss Grace, open up, please! I have a telegraph for Mr Alaniz. They left it at the tea room for him a week ago, and Da' said I must deliver it to you, cos you are back now, and I must be fast."

Everything was said without taking a moment to breathe.

Agnes opened the door and took the message from Kathleen. Kathleen peered into the room and caught Diego's eye; she was going nowhere without a tip. Diego passed her a pound note like it was nothing.

Watching the exchange, Agnes realised that if she played her cards right, associating with this foreigner might be a lucrative opportunity. Much as she hated her sister eloping with that man she had just brought home, bold as brass, she would do whatever it took to remain on the right side of them. *I'll bury the hatchet for now.*

"Diego, may I pour you some tea?" she asked politely, with him nodding in response.

Grace was relieved that Agnes seemed to be relenting a little. The small olive branch was welcome. She was petrified that Agnes would never, ever, warm to Diego, never see the good in him, like she did. She pondered why Agnes might be so frosty, in case this glimmer of kindness was all a front.

Perhaps it was just the shock of the news? Or that it was a reminder that there were no potential suitors for her? Or maybe it was missing their wedding? Agnes is a constant worrier, always preparing for the worst case that might ever occur. For her, this must have been the worst way for her sister to get married. After the death of their parents, perhaps she deserved better? Why did I let my heart rule my head again!

Diego played with the note in his hand, delaying opening it, preferring to try to redeem the relationship between Grace and her sister. He was saddened to think that he was the cause of their strife, not realising that the tension between the wise and the wistful sister had run deep since the death of their parents.

The two sisters began to talk about the wedding and the journey up to the glorious Lake District, with Grace speaking in glowing terms about the honeymoon her husband had arranged.

Diego subtly read the note. The telegraph didn't bring good news.

RIOTING IN SPAIN STOP CIVIL WAR IMMINENT STOP RETURN IMMEDIATELY STOP ALL VESSELS REQUESTED BY GOVERNMENT STOP EDUARDO STOP

Spain had been at war with Cuba, fighting for its independence for almost four years. Now there would be war on the mainland. An Italian had been proclaimed king, and many Spaniards plotted his downfall. Tensions between the factions were rising.

Nobody would ever believe the devastation Diego felt in those moments. His eyes dropped. His heart was in his throat. He had just married and only been with his bride for one month. *And now, I am being summoned to Spain so that the government could make use of my precious ships.*

He was furious. Picking up on his mood, Grace took the note and read it as Agnes continued to talk.

"The cottage sounds lovely, Grace, I have always wondered what—"

She was interrupted when a terrified Grace demanded:

"What does this mean, Diego?"

Agnes had the decency to excuse herself and go upstairs, leaving them to talk. With great difficulty, he continued.

"Grace, the political situation in my country is worsening, and the government needs help. I have to return."

"You can't, you just can't! You're my husband! It shouldn't be like this! Can't you stay? They won't come and get you!" stammered Grace.

"I have no choice," said the Spaniard.

"Oh no Diego, this can't be true." she wailed.

"Grace, I have been ordered by the Duke of Madrid to return. I am the owner of a large shipping fleet which they will want to requisition to transport food and ammunition. If I do not return, I'll be executed for treason, and I'll put Eduardo and his family at risk."

She rushed into his arms in a desperate bid to change his mind, to have him stay with her, to keep him safe. She sobbed uncontrollably. For the first time in her life, she couldn't find any joy within her.

Diego held her close and spoke softly in her ear:

"I am your husband, Grace. I'll always return to you. I promise."

She wouldn't let him go. *How can anyone go to fight in a war and promise they will return?*

He tried to unwrap her arms, but she wouldn't let go. He persisted and managed to untangle himself from her grip. He cradled her to his chest, desperate to offer some comfort. His heart was now banging loudly against his ribs.

"Grace, my angel, it will be over soon, and I'll be back. I am not a soldier, I am not at risk, but my country needs my ships to support the war effort."

"Are you sure?" said Grace, wiping her eyes and trying to be brave. "But I love you so much. We have had so little time together, and now you are being snatched away from me."

"I love you too, Grace. I'll provide for you while I am away and I'll always come back for you."

On hearing him leave, Agnes returned downstairs.

Grace spent day after day longing for him. She felt as though her small taste of heaven was a dream, and the beautiful man she had fallen in love with was just a figment of her imagination.

At that point, Grace was not to know the wait would be so long and challenging. The Third Carlist war lasted until 1876. It was four long years that Diego had never anticipated. Worse he had not spent it on his ships, he spent it in gaol. There would be many letters sent between the young lovers before his final release.

9

THE CONFESSION TO MRS MORRIS

Grace realised that she was pregnant a month after Diego left.

When she didn't get her 'monthly visit' she was concerned. She couldn't go to Agnes, who would be furious. *What would my spinster sister know about pregnancy anyway?* Thankfully, her friendly neighbour Jenny Morris had produced four healthy children, and she would be the one to speak to. *I have seldom spoken to Mrs Morris. How on earth will I broach the subject?* Jenny was a very mature, worldly-wise, twenty-five-year-old and the young and dreamy Grace didn't know how she would begin.

"Jenny, you know that Diego and I were married at the courts just over a month ago, yes? It was all very sudden, hence the lack of an invitation. I'm sorry I've not been to see you, but I was on honeymoon. In the Lake—"

"—Yes, Grace, Agnes told me," interrupted Jenny abruptly.

There was a pause, and Jenny knew precisely what Grace was about to say, but pretended she didn't, hoping to spare her feelings.

"I haven't had my monthlies."

"Well, we all know what that means, Gracie, dear. What did you think would happen? Did you think you were immune to pregnancy?"

Grace felt she was about to be chastised for her hasty marriage, and rapid pregnancy, with a man who had left her already (albeit not by his own decision). She needn't have been. Jenny's tone changed, taking on a more maternal supportive air. She knew young Grace was an orphan with no mother to call upon. *Her sister focuses on her work and has little experience with men, let alone pregnancy. The poor girl is clearly in distress.* Her bottom lip was trembling as she waited for Jenny to reassure her and tell her not to worry.

"You'll be fine, lass, women's bodies are built to bear children. More and more babies and mothers are surviving. Well, for those folks with money behind 'em, at least. I am guessing that well-to-do fella of yours has left you with some money?

Them midwives and doctors can do wonderful things these days."

Grace's frown was softening into a smile, and a thankful expression took over.

"Diego is going to be so happy. He loves spending time with Eduardo's children. To have one of his own will mean the world to him."

Jenny smiled.

"You've found a good man, Grace. You've fallen on your feet. Things will work out. You'll see."

"I know—" she trailed off.

It was a bittersweet moment for her. Diego would have been overjoyed, but he was far away, and the letters were getting more infrequent.

A thoughtful Grace returned home, wondering how she would broach the subject with Agnes. The situation was still frosty at home, and her sister's tolerance of it waxed and waned.

Agnes had been running some errands and arrived home after five o'clock. It was the beginning of summer, and even though the sun was still high, the streets were dense with smog and smoke. A permanent twilight seemed to lurk over the slum. Agnes had a substantial change in temperament over the last week or so. She was always firm like her mother, Elsie, had been, but lately, she was downright unpleasant, finding fault with everything Grace did. Her temper became more and more frayed. In their tiny lodgings, there was nowhere for either of them to retreat from the simmering hostility.

The two sisters still shared a bedroom. Grace desperately needed to confide in Agnes. She felt awkward hiding the truth. *Soon, the truth would be out anyway. It's better that I tell her than she works it out for herself. Tonight is the night that I must confess my condition to her.*

That evening as they were lying in their beds after a long and tiring day, Grace finally mustered the courage to say something. Her timid voice wafted through from the other side of the curtain.

"Agnes," she began, "I need to tell you something. I am— pregnant."

She was terrified of Agnes's reply and rightly so.

"I knew it!" said Agnes venomously. "I knew it. Now, what are we going to do with you?"

"I am not an invalid," replied Grace "ladies do not need anything 'doing' with them when they are pregnant. Plenty of other women manage."

"But, if anything happens, it'll be me who's supposed to look after you!"

"No, Agnes, Diego has left enough money for me to look after myself for a year. If I have to stop work, we'll manage," answered Grace, indignantly, disappointed that Agnes had so little faith in her husband and his ability to provide.

Agnes brightened up a little at the disclosure of the exact amount of money. Until then it had been 'some', now it was 'a year's worth'. Then, she resumed her attack.

"When were you going to tell me about just how much money you have?" she asked.

"I was keeping it for a rainy day, Agnes, when we really needed it. I've been able to work. I've pulled my weight."

"That's going to make everything OK, is it? What happens when you have to look after the child? What will your rich keeper do then? Send even more money?" replied Agnes spitefully.

"Diego is my husband," retaliated Grace. "He is not my keeper!"

"You will be lucky if you ever see him again. What did he ever see in a useless slum-dweller like you? He could have had the pick of the most beautiful ladies in Spain as a successful merchant." mocked Agnes.

Grace was overcome with sadness. Tears streamed down her face.

"I thought that you would be happy for us," said Grace.

There was no reply from the other side of the curtain.

10

SEND FOR MRS STEPHENS

Grace, the angel of the meadow, now became the subject of intense gossip. The common people who used to have time for her, soon made her life a living misery, jealous of her rich husband.

She was dismayed to find the source of the scurrilous comments was eight-year-old Kathleen, a girl to whom Diego had bestowed some generous thanks. She had gained the attention of the whole street when she relayed in detail the Spaniard's first arrival and how he had met Grace. She embellished the tale further by telling them about the weeks of meeting in the tea room. She fibbed about seeing them holding hands under the table because she knew little white lies like that were an easy way to boost her own popularity. The old crones in the tenement courtyards hung onto every word the child told them. They would have no doubt loved to hear that Diego had tipped Kathleen with generous amounts of cash, had she not consciously omitted to tell them about it.

For such a young person, Kathleen was a tremendous busy body. She was proficient at the art of manipulation and brilliant at intelligence gathering. Eavesdropping outside Grace's house, she heard Grace and Agnes arguing about the baby. Within one hour the entire row knew Grace was pregnant and by the end of the week most of Angel Meadow.

What was most frustrating for Grace was that nobody was interested in the genuine love between the couple, just the salacious details.

"He looked very—rich." a furtive Kathleen told Ma Smith up the street.

"Do you think they are married, lass?"

"Me Da says they are," she answered like a gossipy little washerwoman. "And, one of the ladies who does cleaning work at the registry office said she saw them leaving together early one morning."

"Then why is she still 'ere? Why is she not with that new 'usband of hers?"

"Dunno, Ma, but I'll find out. You can trust me."

"'Ere lass, buy ya'sel somefin' for yer troubles. You keep me informed now, you hear?"

Kathleen smiled as she took the tuppence. It would buy her another handful of sweets.

And so, the story grew. A wealthy Spaniard had whisked Grace away and married her at the courts. He took her away to the countryside and had his way—many times—then when he was bored, he abandoned her. He was decent enough to dump her back at the Meadow, where she was soon going to have his baby.

> "Well, who did she think she was anyhow?" was the general consensus. "She got too big for her breeches again. It was doomed from the start. A gentleman would never want a slum girl for anything more than a drunken fumble."

Agnes did nothing to dissuade anybody from their horrid opinions.

Thankfully, Coggan, the tea shop owner was an angel. Diego would still forward his letters there. John seemed to be the only person who had a kind word for Grace. She loved collecting the letters. It was the highlight of her week, the only thing that lifted her spirits in the horrors of the slum. Now, it was all the more horrible as those around began to ridicule and ostracise her. As a person who tended to see the good in people rather than the bad, she struggled to understand why they were so eager to be so cruel.

There would be a letter for Grace every week. She would also collect money transmitted to the bank using the new, magical wire transfer system, sent to her by Eduardo. She was grateful no one in the slums knew about it. It helped keep the money secret.

Grace put some of her income towards the house. The majority, however, she hid in her sewing box, far from the eyes of her sister. It was not that she wouldn't share, but she was planning to move away from Angel Meadow after the baby was born, and that was the nest egg that would make her escape possible. Angel Meadow was no place to raise a child, and Diego also insisted that it was time to move to somewhere safer.

Diego's response to hearing Grace was pregnant was beautiful.

To my darling Grace,

I know that our child will be as beautiful as you.

I love you with all my heart, and cannot wait to have you in my arms once more.

We will be together soon; I am convinced of it.

Your loving husband,

Diego

At night she would lie in the little room with the curtain drawn between her and Agnes. She would read his letters again and again by the flickering candlelight. How she longed to be with him where she felt safe.

Month by month, her tummy grew, but in comparison with the other pregnant women about her, she seemed huge.

"Agnes, there must be something wrong," she said eventually.

"I can ask Mrs Stephens to come and see you, but you will have to pay," answered Agnes in a very matter of fact tone.

Grace didn't dare touch her savings, which was their ticket out of Angel Meadow. She sensed that Diego would be absent for quite some time and didn't want to waste a penny of it. The civil war on the Spanish peninsula showed no signs of being settled one way or the other, and she felt she would have to manage alone for quite some time to come.

"Agnes, you can give me some extra sewing, I don't mind working into the night."

"Good," said Agnes, because I have nothing for you.

The next morning, Agnes did the first helpful thing for her sister in quite some time and arranged for Mrs Stephens to visit. A few days later, at about ten o'clock in the morning, she appeared at their doorway. Agnes answered and directed the visitor upstairs to their bedroom.

She was a small, sallow woman with crepe-like wrinkled skin. Her blue eyes were sunken into her face, and her teeth protruded like ugly, ramshackle gravestones. Despite her strange appearance, reassuringly, she was carrying a small doctor's bag and had an air of professionalism about her. Grace was not sure of what to expect, but the woman was kind and took the trouble to explain how babies developed.

"How far do you think you are?" she asked Grace, looking at her belly.

"I think about seven months," Grace answered.

"And, what is bothering you, child, are you feeling unwell?"

"No, I am fine, but my stomach is so much larger than the other women around me," she answered vaguely. "And there is a lot of movement."

"Ok my dear, let's lift up that dress and take a feel."

Grace lay on her bed and pulled up her dress and petticoats.

Mrs Stephens began pushing and prodding.

"Are you sure you're seven months gone?"

"Yes" answered Grace earnestly.

"From what I can feel, Grace, there are two babies. You are going to have twins."

"Twins. I've never had one baby before, and now I'm having two at once." she howled, pleased the children seemed healthy but anxious all the same.

"Try not to worry yourself, Grace," answered Mrs Stephens, "You look fit and energetic. You are nice and young, and it seems you are eating properly. Your babies should be due at the end of January. I'll visit again next month, and we will discuss your confinement."

"Thank you, Mrs Stephens," answered Grace.

She didn't know what all of the terminology meant, she was just happy to hear that all was well, though a bit daunted at the thought of giving birth to two babies.

"Agnes, Mrs Stephens says that I am going to have twins," said Grace joyfully, hoping for some reassurance from her sister.

Agnes ignored her. She was secretly glad when Diego's letters dried up. *I hope he's dead. It will serve him right for taking advantage of a young woman like that.* Grace put the lack of letters down to the conditions of his imprisonment, making communication difficult, and not anything worse. It was the only way to cope with the silence.

As time passed the gossip about Grace began to subside as new scandals came to light to take its place.

A few close neighbours sensed that Agnes was not inclined to kindness with her sister, and put considerable effort into supporting Grace. They could see she was struggling with the disappearance of her husband's regular letters. No one but the fraught mother-to-be knew the regular money had also dried up.

One of her most ardent supporters was Jenny Morris. Although the Morris's lived in total chaos with eleven people in their meagre lodgings, every evening after work, Grace would be welcomed to their kitchen for a cup of tea. Her support was invaluable. Grace hung off Jenny's every word as she described what to expect during the last stages of her pregnancy and labour. She did her best to allay Grace of any fears she may have and promised to support her during the birth.

There wouldn't be long to wait. A few weeks later, Grace went into labour at eight o'clock in the evening, Jenny asked Agnes to send for Mrs Stephens, who arrived in haste.

11

WHAT TO DO WITH GRACE

"I think these two will make an appearance tomorrow morning at about eleven," announced a confident Mrs Stephens.

A horrified Grace looked at the clock. *That's fifteen hours away!*

"Well, Denny, I've 'ad four children, and I think they'll come faster. Grace 'asn't got time to lie around all day." she said with a laugh, seeing Grace's worried expression.

The first-time mother hoped Jenny was right, and thankfully she was. Six hours later, at two in the morning, Grace had been delivered of two beautiful little girls. She received a lot of attention which annoyed Agnes. In fact, everyone seemed to receive more attention than her.

The midwife was delighted that the birth had progressed so well.

The two little babies were precious. One twin was fair-haired like Grace, and the other had inherited Diego's darker Moorish colouring.

"Mother and father would have loved them dearly," said Grace, running the back of her curled forefinger along their peachy, cherub-like cheeks.

"Yes." Agnes agreed reluctantly. "They would have."

Grace stared at her daughters for quite some time, struggling to come up with suitable names.

"What shall we call them, Agnes? They are so different."

"Anything you like—just not my name," replied a spiteful sister, her hostility returning now Jenny and Mrs Stephens had said their goodbyes.

Grace ignored her nastiness

"Well, I think Bianca is a Spanish name that means white—and then Ruby after my wedding ring. That will be perfect." murmured the thoughtful mother.

If she had been wearing her wedding ring, she would have toyed with it at that point, but the threat of scuttlers meant she had chosen not to wear it ever since Diego left. It was kept safe in the sewing box.

She loved the babies dearly, and it was a joyous time. However, living without Diego was getting more and more depressing as time went on.

Although the birth had gone well, the postpartum period was terrifying. Grace quickly succumbed to a terrible fever. For three days she became desperately ill, barely able to get out of bed. There was an awful stench from the blood she was passing. Things were clearly amiss.

Worried about the expense, Agnes waited quite a while before she called the doctor to the house. She was secretly worried she had left it too long. The day before, Jenny found two wet nurses for the babies concerned that Grace was too weak to nourish them properly.

Mrs Stephens was in attendance when the doctor arrived. He swiftly began his examination. After a few minutes, he shared his findings.

"She has an acute infection." deduced Dr Simmonds.

"But how, doctor? She did so well with the birth, and I thoroughly checked her over afterwards?" said Mrs Stephens.

"I believe that a small piece of placenta is still attached to her womb. Sometimes it attaches too firmly in places and cannot be fully expelled. A portion of it has begun to putrefy inside her. Sometimes it can be manipulated out of position. If not, I have an instrument, and I can attempt to remove it, but there are no guarantees."

He reached inside his bag and picked up a long thin tool with a small loop for scraping at the end of it. The two women onlookers left the room leaving Mrs Stephens and Dr Simmonds to conduct the work required. Downstairs, even cold-hearted Agnes became distraught at the thought of losing her last close relative. Grace was not her usual self at all. Everyone who saw her became gravely concerned. Jenny was furious. She had warmed to Grace, such a gentle and thoughtful soul. *Perhaps you should have been less spiteful to your sister before, Agnes? It's a bit too late to show concern now.*

Mrs Stephens hurried out after asking Agnes for yet more money for something from the pharmacy. This time, with Grace's condition deteriorating by the hour, she didn't complain. On her return, the midwife scurried upstairs with a great sense of urgency. Moments later, Dr Simmonds called the two women upstairs. They arrived as he was rinsing his blood-stained hands in a white porcelain bowl. The smell was awful, and Jenny opened the bedroom window briefly to help it dissipate. Then, thoughtfully, she slid it closed to keep Grace warm. Mrs Stephens was plumping Grace's pillows, trying to make her a little more comfortable. It didn't seem to be doing any good. Dr Simmonds gave an update.

"Mrs Stephens and I have removed the matter from her womb and rinsed her with a mild solution of carbolic soap. I have prescribed some medicine, but the disease may have taken too strong a hold. What she needs most of all now is bed rest. I'll be back tomorrow morning to check on her."

The three women took turns through the night to look after Grace and the babies. She was delirious, her head lolling about and her eyes rolling, calling, begging for Diego. Grace slipped into a coma the following day at ten in the morning. When the doctor arrived, there was nothing he could do to help. She passed away at noon.

Agnes responded like her mother the night her husband was killed; she didn't feel grief. Fury was uppermost in her mind. Everybody was her enemy now: Grace for marrying without her knowledge, Diego for being absent, Mrs Stephens for not being more thorough and the doctor for not saving her.

Her final resting place was at St Michael's with an unmarked grave near her mother and father. It rained that day, but a lot of people attended the funeral, including John and Kathleen Coggan from the tea room. Kath took in every detail. She would be relied on to repeat the story in full to her eager audiences in all the tenement courtyards later that day.

Agnes left as soon as the service was over, only attending to avoid being the centre of any more gossiping. After a cup of tea in her lonely back-to-back, as the twins emitted ear-splitting screams at the top of their voices, she set about removing every trace of Grace from her home apart from two things—the sewing box of money and her expensive ruby wedding ring.

12

THE UNWELCOME RESPONSIBILITY

The twins were now four years old. Bianca was almost identical to Grace. Her tousled little blonde head bobbed about the house as she bounced with joy. Bianca was affectionate and friendly, which made her easy to please. She could spend hours playing by herself, inheriting the same disposition as Arthur and Grace. She would always be a personality who straddled the joyous world of fantasy and the grim world of reality.

But Ruby was the opposite in nature and in looks. She had dark hair and dark skin, a clear display of her Spanish heritage, often mistaken as a gipsy. She was brooding and challenging, asking endless questions. The most notable thing was her fierce protectiveness of her sister.

The girls were in Agnes's care. At first, Agnes coped reasonably well with life in the slum. However, with the birth of the babies and the death of her sister, she had suffered a considerable financial loss. Diego's letters stopped some time ago. She had found the money in the sewing box, but it had long since been spent. Things had become desperate. Agnes was forced to move into a single room in a tenement building.

Grace's ruby wedding ring had been pawned to help make ends meet, and the money had kept them going for two years. The last year had been hellish with nowhere near enough money to live on. The sleepless nights spent looking after the twins had exhausted her. The hourly interruptions to care for them were disruptive.

The quality and productivity of her sewing suffered as a consequence. The better-paid society work dried up, and she was back living hand-to-mouth with the unskilled basic repair work she had done as a young girl. The twins were full time work, and she couldn't afford a carer for them. Jenny Morris had helped her when they were still in the back-to-back, living in the tenement, for Agnes there was no help at all.

The tenements were an undesirable place to live. They bordered the putrid River Irk, which bubbled up with toxic waste from the cotton mills, foundries, tanneries and whatever junk the people threw into it. Overflowing sewage coursed down the hill, through the streets of the tenements, finding the easiest route to the lowest point.

Like a cauldron of disease-bearing bacteria, it was a source of many a case of typhoid and cholera.

Walking through the streets was a nightmare as skirts and shoes were embedded with stinking mud. Cart wheel's splashed filth up clothing as they rumbled by.

It was a living hell. A few journalists under police escort had revealed the horror in their penny dreadful tabloid newspapers. They reported Manchester, and Angel Meadow, in particular, was the worst place to live in the whole of industrialised Europe.

The air pollution was overbearing, resulting in terrible lung diseases. Relief would only come from leaving for the country for a few weeks of breathing uncontaminated air. A possibility beyond the means of all the residents. The streets retained their permanent dusk-like quality through the day. Angel Meadow existed in an eerie black haze that outsiders were too terrified to enter.

Darkness of another kind also descended on Angel Meadow in the form of gangs. Since the death of Arthur, the removal of Davie Gleech had changed nothing. The flourishing underworld now dominated the existence of all the residents. Terror reigned on the streets, and the day time visual horror of squalor was exacerbated by the night time invisible threat of the ever-present violence. Anybody was a target, young or old, sick or well, male or female.

Agnes looked about the dismal room she shared with the twins. She was trapped because of her sister's stupid mistake. It was a cold and wet evening outside, the cobbles slippery with coal dust. Wet washing hung across the room, exacerbating the mould problem within. Ruby stood at a small bucket of laundry, moving it around with a long wooden dolly to podge it clean. Bianca sat on Agnes's lap while she drank a cup of tea.

"Ruby—Ruby! Make sure you wring those out properly after you have washed them, or I'll make you do it all again. I do not want the floor dripping wet," reprimanded Agnes, even though the young child was doing the job correctly and not a drop of water had been sloshed on the floor.

Ruby continued what she was doing as her aunt glared at her, paying no attention to the commands being issued. Ruby was much wiser than her years with a built-in survivor's instinct. *What riles me so much about that wretched child? She is pretty enough and more intelligent than Bianca, but she still vexes me?* To Agnes, it seemed as though Ruby knew her aunt hated her, but she didn't care one jot. Ruby had an indifference to Agnes, and she couldn't bear the insolence of it.

Riled by the child's lack of response, Agnes continued:

"—and you can take out the slops when you are done."

Ruby finished with the washing. The slops bucket was half her size. Agnes put it outside their lodging door for her, only because she didn't want the dirty water sloshing onto the floor inside their room. Ruby struggled down the deep tenement stairs, bucket in hand. It was heavy, and each bump down a step spilt a bit of the stinking bilge. Finally, she reached the front steps of the tenement, walked a few paces and poured the contents into an open gutter running down the street, straight into the river. She walked a hundred yards to the water pump in the street and rinsed out the bucket.

Constable McGregor watched the little girl lug the heavy pail up the street. He shook his head. He knew all the children in the neighbourhood, and the story was the same—drudgery from the day that they could walk. Their parents had given up on life, taking to the bottle to escape, but Ruby's case was unusual. Her spinster aunt was raising her. Agnes was a beautiful, steely self-suffi-cient woman. Constable McGregor wasn't sure of the exact situation. Agnes was a very private woman. *They seem to be keeping their head above water. Just.*

When the tiny child was halfway back to her home. He took the bucket from her small olive-skinned hand.

"Och, Ruby," he smiled, "let me help ya along with that."

The Scots bobby had a soft spot for the serious little girl. Some of the brats in the Meadow were poorly mannered of course, but Ruby had a dignity about her that trans-cended her four years.

"Thank you, Sir," she answered, giving him a rare smile.

"How is your Aunt Agnes, lassie?" he asked, for the sake of making conversation.

"She is fine, Sir."

"And your wee little sister, Bianca?" he continued

"She is fine, Sir. She's a bit smaller than me, but she bides well."

Constable McGregor's big heart wanted to break. This poor little girl was so protective of her sister.

"Come on, lassie. Here's ya door," he said, giving the bucket back to her. He reached into his pocket and grinned. "And here's some toffee for ya troubles."

"Thank you, Mister!" she smiled, then skipped off to take the two flights of stairs to Agnes's room.

Ruby entered the room and went straight to her sister, who was lying on her bed about to sleep. She climbed in next to her. Bianca put her little arm around Ruby. The twins had slept together from the day they were born and hadn't spent one night apart. They snuggled against each other.

With her usual cruel streak, Agnes tried to separate them that night by putting Bianca into bed with her. Bianca screamed blue murder for Ruby, which meant no one got any sleep. Agnes was forced to back down and let her return to her sister. Ruby said nothing, she just watched it all.

Bianca stopped screaming the instant she was reunited with her sister. Agnes felt that Ruby was watching her, convinced that the child was laughing in her smug little mind.

Agnes walked over to her and looked into her big brown eyes.

"You are too big for your boots," she whispered menacingly. "Do you know what I do to little girls who are too big for their boots?"

As usual, the nonchalant child failed to respond, and it infuriated her aunt further. Agnes took Ruby's arm and pinched it as hard as she could. The little girl made no sound. Agnes shook the infant violently, her head thrown this way and that. Her bony fingers pinched her harder still. *What do I have to do to make her scream in pain?* Furious, she clambered into her bed, cold and alone. *I hate that child.* After a few hours, she would be wracked with guilt because of her behaviour. *What on earth would my parents or Grace say if they could see me behave so violently towards the child?* It was an endless cycle of guilt and abuse. Exhausted, she fell asleep.

Ruby lay with a protective arm over her little sister. They were warm and snug. The abuse had hurt, and now when no-one could see, a tear ran down her little face. She rubbed her arm where it had been pinched to soothe it. Then, she clenched her teeth and tightened her fists. Somehow, Ruby was astute enough to know that she had more power over Agnes when she refused to speak or cry.

The days were an endless repetitive sequence. If Agnes had not been stuck with the children, she could be working in well-to-do Chester for her society dressmaker. The weeks she spent there around the time Grace married that bounder Diego Alaniz had been one of her happiest and most lucrative times in her life. *Oh, to rewind the clock.*

Agnes began to take a drink. At the start, it was a thimble of whisky at night in her tea, just a little something to take the edge off. The constant stress to provide was taking its toll on her. She was depressed, trapped, and the vision she had for her life was extinguished by acquiring two children she didn't want.

She would have to be completely heartless to send them to an orphanage. She could never do that to blonde little Bianca who reminded her so much of Grace. But Ruby, that was different. Ruby was a constant reminder of a better life. If Grace had lived, maybe they would all be living in Spain, in a beautiful home, with nothing to worry about. Every time she saw Ruby, with her dark Spanish looks, Agnes was filled with hate for Diego Alaniz. It was his selfishness that had robbed her of her one last living relative and left her saddled with his offspring. *Why on earth didn't he come back to collect them? He must be dead by now, or he would have been back, surely?*

Thanks to the regular beatings doled out by Agnes, Ruby was covered with bumps and bruises, but that was not unusual for children in Angel Meadow; nobody cared about trivialities like that. Everybody was too busy surviving.

Agnes moved onto gin and drank more and more. By eight o'clock, most evenings, she was passed out. Ruby loved the hours when Agnes collapsed stone drunk— they were peaceful and pain-free. Ruby and Bianca would crawl under the covers. They would talk, giggle and keep each other warm. On those nights, the little bed had the two most cheerful children in Angel Meadow, despite Ruby being the bane of her aunt's life.

Agnes would awake in the morning, hungover, bitter and hopeless. The worse she felt, the more chores she palmed off on Ruby. Sometimes, those chores allowed Ruby to escape the confines of the room.

Her greatest adventure was being sent to the market. Everywhere in Angel Meadow was miserable, but it allowed her to see people and new things. The little child was so quiet and unobtrusive that she was virtually invisible, except to Constable McGregor who always kept an eye on her like a real-life guardian angel.

The bobby always wondered what had happened to her father. He remembered the man clearly and knew his commitment to Grace. Kathleen's gossip made sure everyone knew the ins-and-outs of her life. *It seems unlikely that a gentleman like him would discard his children if they had been born in wedlock? And Kathleen said they appeared to have married for love? Will he ever return?*

He wished more for the little girl, but she was in the care of Agnes. He had worked these streets for many years. There were hundreds of ragged little children, all living in the same harsh circumstances. Some were destroyed at a very young age, but he had a good feeling about Ruby. She had a robustness about her that meant she would be fine.

"Good evening, Miss Ruby," he said jovially as she passed, tipping his bobby's hat to greet her.

"Evenin', Sir," she answered, looking very serious.

"And what is your errand this late in the day?" he asked her.

"I'm fetching my aunt some tea from the market. She likes a cuppa when she finishes work," she replied hastily, aware that if she didn't hurry back, Agnes would take the strap to her.

"You better be quick then, Ruby, it's getting dark. No dilly-dallying. Off you trot." He pretended to be fierce with her.

She smiled at him. He couldn't fool her.

"Come, lassie, I have a boiled sweet for you. There you go. You enjoy it."

"Thank you, Mister," she smiled. This time he got a wave too.

Ruby ran home as fast as her legs could carry her. She rushed into the room, relieved to see that Agnes was already asleep when she got back. She put the kettle on the little stove and made some tea, then cut a hunk of bread and a chunk of cheese for her and Bianca. They sat under their blankets while they feasted.

Bianca made up a story of them being in the woods having tea with the fairies. Ruby listened carefully, she loved Bianca's fantastical stories. But more so, she loved the peace that came when Agnes lay snoring on her bed.

Ruby developed an exceptional respect for alcohol. From a young age, she saw it as a means to an end. She found great benefit in watching people get drunk and fall over. If you could remain invisible until they passed out, you were home and dry and would avoid a beating. She learned to never get in the way of Agnes and her glass. She never caused a commotion when the bottle came out, in fact, she welcomed it. She remained as quiet as a mouse not wanting to distract Agnes from consuming as much as necessary to lose consciousness. The sooner Aunt Agnes fell asleep on her bed, the sooner Ruby could relax.

5

THE BLESSING OF THE EMPTY GIN BOTTLE

The day was as cold and bitter as Agnes. Water was leaking in through the window frame. She had tried to stuff newspaper into the sides to prevent the wind and rain getting through but to no avail.

It was a wet and soggy mess with dark, inky water running down the wall beneath it. The little coal stove was making no difference to the freezing temperature, and the three of them were dressed in every piece of clothing that they owned.

It was eleven o'clock in the morning, but it was black as night as usual outside. There had been three deaths in the tenement this week, two children and one man. No disease was involved only the cold; their weakened bodies frozen to death. The room was starting to stink of human waste, and the slop bucket was filling. It was no use putting it into the corridor, someone would knock it over, and it would seep under the door. Agnes was one step away from giving up, so she reached for her gin bottle hidden under her bed, unscrewed the top and hoped to drink down the fiery liquid. It would slide down her gullet like hot lava and hit her cold, empty stomach like a rock. A few more minutes, and she would feel better. Today, however, the bottle was empty. She climbed back under the blanket.

Ruby walked over to the small range cooker and put on the pot to boil water.

"I'll have tea," ordered Agnes.

Ruby's little fingers were red and swollen, covered with chilblains. Mrs Morris told her to massage her hands with sheep fat to keep them moist. If there was any available, Ruby would rub it her hands and Bianca's, but of late, there was none. She saw the slops needed emptying and sooner or later Agnes would send her to do it. *I'd better do it sooner rather than later.*

She and Bianca drank the steaming hot tea which warmed them up. They had a piece of stale bread and shared half a potato from the dinner last night, a respite from the gnawing hunger for a few minutes. She put on a bonnet and coat, wrapped a scarf around her neck, then picked up the slops bucket and headed for the door.

"Can I come with you?" asked Bianca.

"No," replied Ruby, "it is far too cold out there, go back to bed before you catch yer death."

Ruby headed for the slippery stairway, it stank of human faeces and urine. She slipped down the first three steps, willing to take the pain of falling rather than dropping the bucket. A kind man helped her up and carried the bucket to the door for her.

"Thank you, Sir." She said as he carefully passed it back.

"No problem, Miss," he answered, politely tipping his hat and smiling.

Ruby put him on the list of nice people that she kept in her head.

She poured the contents into the midden in the courtyard and headed to the water pump a street away. She dodged the toxic puddles and managed to keep her balance on the treacherously slippy cobbles. She rinsed the bucket and returned to the flat, her shoes congealed with a mixture of mud and excrement.

"Get outside and clean those boots off, now!" raged Agnes "I don't want you stinking out the inside of my house."

Ruby turned around obediently and returned to the water pump to clean her boots. She tiptoed along stepping on the highest spots on her route home to try to keep her feet clean. The hem of her dress was a disaster, and

Agnes made her wash it with carbolic soap the minute she got back.

After that, Ruby was forced to sweep the floor of their lodgings and dust and tidy everything within reach. Ruby was pleased that for once, it looked a bit neater, at least for a while. There would be no respite from the chores. Agnes continued to order her around, enjoying feeling superior over her loathsome niece.

"I need you to fetch bread, shortening and cabbage from the market,"

Ruby got up, took the money and headed for the market, her boots getting dirty again. She put her basket over her arm and ran. It kept her warm. Breathing in the stench from the street was awful, but it was still better than the atmosphere back at home with Agnes.

While Ruby ran her errand, back at the lodgings, there was a loud knock on the door which startled Agnes. She didn't have visitors anymore now her sewing business was failing. These days, most of the garments needing repair she collected herself. *Who can this be?* She shuffled over to the door and opened it to a well-dressed man. She looked at him for a while, her reactions slowed because of the surprise. Then she placed the face that greeted her. It was Diego Alaniz. She felt dizzy and sick at the sight of him. It had been so many years since the last letter, she was genuinely convinced he was dead.

"Good day, Agnes," he said to her formally.

"—Diego. It's you! You're—alive!" she stuttered.

"Agnes, I have come to collect Grace and the baby. May I come in?"

He tried to look over her shoulder into the room. He was beside himself with anguish, desperate to see his beloved family after all this time. Agnes opened the door and signalled for him to come in with a sweep of her arm.

Despite Ruby's efforts to tidy it, the room was dismal. *This is no place to raise a child.* He was convinced it was worse than the hellish slums in Barcelona. He was ashamed that the abandonment of his wife and child meant they ended up living in such squalor. It was nothing like the proud, neat little back-to-back he had left them in. The tenement building inside and out was pure horror. His eyes scoured the dingy room and settled on a small girl with tousled blonde hair and big blue eyes.

"Is that her? Is that my daughter?".

He looked at Agnes for confirmation.

"Yes, her name is Bianca," said Agnes

Diego smiled.

"That's a lovely name for you, my dear. It's perfect and so are you," he said, admiring the little blonde cherub before him.

She was beautiful, identical to Grace. He was besotted with her at first sight.

"Hola, Bianca," he said in his Spanish accent, "It's me. Diego. I am your father."

Bianca gave him a charming but shy smile.

"How old are you?" he asked her trying to forge a bond.

"Five," she said, holding up her hand, fingers and thumbs outstretched.

Diego was so fascinated with the little girl that for a moment, he forgot about Grace.

"And where is your mother, sweetheart?" he asked with an excited smile.

"Aunty Agnes says that my mummy is with the angels," Bianca answered him, her eyes big and serious.

Diego hoped she was mistaken. He glanced up at Agnes with a questioning frown.

"Grace is dead," said Agnes, making no effort to soften the blow. "She got an infection, and she died."

It was only the hope of fetching Grace that kept him alive during his long hard years of imprisonment. He had built such a detailed picture of the reunion. *And now there was nothing?* He sat down on a dangerously rickety chair. It was as though he was winded and couldn't recover.

"Where did you bury her? I need to be close to her."

"At St Michael's Flags up the 'ill. With ma and pa." she answered.

"I want to go there, please."

"There is nothing to see. The last flood caused another landslide, and the coffins and bodies were washed down the slope. They had to be moved, and some were incinerated," answered Agnes, being very matter-of-fact about it.

"So, there is nothing left of her?"

"Nothing."

Diego didn't want to crumple in front of Agnes or Bianca and left the room, closing the door softly behind him. He went down the stairs and crossed the foul street to stand under the grocer's awning out of the rain. Tears stung the rims of his eyes like acid as he fought to keep them back. It was the darkest moment of his life. His body began to shudder from the cold, and he had a heaviness in his chest.

He went back to the room. Agnes watched him pick up the little girl.

"I am going to take you far away from here, little Bianca. We are going to sail on a massive steamship, and I am going to take you to Spain. To a big white villa, just like the castles pretty princesses live in. You will never be cold or hungry again."

Bianca liked this man, and she loved the story. She smiled, yelling:

"When? When?"

"Agnes, please have the two of you ready by noon tomorrow. I'll send a cab and driver to collect you, and I'll be taking you both to Spain."

Agnes couldn't believe her ears—she was to be included in the child's new life.

Diego returned to the Grand Hotel in Manchester, taking the staircase to his usual suite on the fifth floor. The hotel lived up to its name, designed as the ultimate luxury for the elite classes. But Diego saw nothing. He could appreciate nothing, and it meant nothing to him.

Eduardo Garcia waited impatiently for Diego in their suite. He stared out at the stair rod rain lashing against the bay window, wondering what was happening. He didn't want to spoil Diego's reunion with Grace and the precious child, feeling his presence would intrude on the gathering. He knew that for Diego, the last few years were the worst he had ever experienced. Now it was time for his best friend to have the joy he had stayed alive for. Not in all their time at sea had Eduardo ever witnessed Diego as tormented as he had been in prison. His heart ached for his family more than the freedom of the open ocean.

Eduardo heard the handle rattle and the door to the suite swing open. Diego collapsed into the chair opposite, looking drained. He didn't bother to remove his hat and coat.

"You look drenched. You've been gone quite a while," said Eduardo.

"Yes, I had to find a new residence. Grace moved from the back-to-back where I last saw her. John at the tea shop was able to help. I sent my driver in to ask about her whereabouts."

Diego said nothing. He stared at the floor. Water dripped from his coat tails and walking cane. A puddle started to form on the immaculate marble tiles. He had wiped his shoes, but they were still grubby from the streets of the Meadow. Smears of dirt formed as he shuffled his feet, trying to get comfortable, and failing.

Eduardo knew there was no point forcing the conversation. Diego would speak in his own time. He walked over to the drinks trolley and poured Diego a large cognac to warm him.

He put the glass down next to Diego, now in a trance, tapping the floor with his cane. Softly, at first, tap, tap, tap, then harder and louder. The knocking sound reached a crescendo culminating in him standing up, lifting the cane above his head, then whipping it down, smashing the crystal cognac glass into smithereens. Eduardo ran for cover in a far corner of the room, amazed at the sight before him. With an almighty second whack, Diego's cane smashed in two when it hit the side table. *He is usually such a calm and measured man. What on earth has happened? Was Grace forced to go with another man thinking her husband was dead? Did God choose to take the child?*

Diego stood in the middle of a floor, breathless from his violent outburst. *It's all my fault!*

Eduardo rushed to him, trying to offer his friend some brotherly solace, but Diego pushed him away furiously.

"Diego, my friend, I am here for you. Please, tell me what has happened?"

"—Grace is dead, and only the child is alive. Bianca is a perfect, miniature version of her mother. Oh, how the child reminds me of her. My heart bleeds. How can my dearest Grace be gone?"

"My dearest friend—I am so sorry."

"I should never have left them in this godforsaken hole. I was under such pressure from the war committee to get our ships back to Spain. Why did months have to turn into years? They were the only things I lived for."

"I have no words, my friend," he said, and he didn't. Carmen would have known what to say, how to soothe, but Eduardo Garcia was a man with none of those skills.

"I want her back," he screamed, "I want her back! Back!"

Diego walked to the drinks trolley and picked up a full bottle of whisky. He thundered towards his bedroom, slamming the door behind him. When Eduardo checked on him an hour later, he was passed out on the bed, still wearing his damp clothes, with the empty bottle lying beside him on the covers. With considerable difficulty, Eduardo wrestled Diego out of his clothes and covered him with a blanket. *Sleep, my dear friend. How I wish I could save you from this heartbreak.*

The dawn broke over Manchester. Diego's mouth was parched, and his stomach angry. His head hammered. In the distance, he saw the black chimneys belching smoke and raining it down upon Angel Meadow. He hated the place more than ever. His child was in that hell hole, and today he would rescue her from it.

He quaffed two strong cups of coffee. They were bitter and horrid but did the trick. He had lacked energy, but now he had just enough to get started. Severely hungover, he struggled to stay focused on his task or to follow Eduardo's conversation, but he did his best.

"Let me come too, Diego?"

"I am too ashamed. How can I have been so stupid to abandon my family? It's my fault Grace is dead!"

"You had no choice at the time. You had orders from the government, and you received the note a week late because of your honeymoon. There was no time to make a proper plan. You had to flee."

"I thought it would only be a few months—"

"—We all did."

"Eduardo, I love—loved— Grace so much. I waited so many years for her. I envied your happiness and your family. And then when I got it, I made the most terrible decision that killed my wife." spluttered Diego, brimming with grief and guilt.

"You still have a daughter. Grace lives on in her. You need to be strong. She needs you more than ever. Go and fetch her. Look after her. Protect her. I'll come with you."

But Diego was paralysed with sorrow and shame. He couldn't mobilise himself and couldn't get his thoughts in order.

Eventually, it would be Eduardo who took the lead. He fetched Diego's hat and coat. *Better not get you a new cane today, my friend.* Diego had not shaved and looked exhausted, but there was nothing Eduardo could do about that. He was sure Diego would have taken better care of his appearance on such an important day, but now was not the time for such polite niceties. Where they were going, men conducted themselves very differently.

He steered Diego out of the hotel and down onto the street. Their driver waited a few paces from the luxurious frontage of the Grand. They climbed into the cab. Diego slouched in the corner with his hat pulled low over his eyes. He stared ahead of him, trapped in thought.

"Do you want to take her body back to Spain with us?" asked Eduardo kindly.

"We can't," whispered Diego.

"Why not?"

He explained about the terrible landslide to his horrified friend.

"And, Agnes, her sister? What do you plan for her?"

"She is a very kind and strong woman. Despite the difficult circumstances of being a lone guardian, she has done her best. She has cared for Bianca all this time. She is the reason my daughter is still alive. She is coming with us to Spain."

6

THE WELL-TIMED ERRAND

Agnes couldn't overcome the desire to lose Ruby—for good. Her heart began to race as she plotted. *When Bianca asks for Ruby, I shall say she is an imaginary friend.* At last, she could rid herself of the insolent child who had no fear of her, nor respect. For the cruel aunt, it was a pleasant thought.

Since the unexpected visit yesterday, Agnes had not stopped fantasising about her new life in Barcelona. *Surely Diego wouldn't have his beloved sister-in-law work as a servant in his house? Finally, I shall have the place in society I deserve. I'll give up the bottle and pull myself together. I still have the looks to capture any man's heart. I'll mould myself into a fine lady—take elocution lessons—study etiquette. Then, I'll weave myself into Barcelona society. I shall be an exquisite English rose amongst the jaded Spanish thorns.*

At a quarter to twelve, Agnes gave Ruby the slops bucket and sent her off just as she had planned it in the night. As the girl turned to leave, her aunt yelled:

"While you're at that, take the soap and scrub out that bucket. I want it spotlessly clean."

As soon as the coast was clear, she dressed Bianca and herself in their Sunday best. Twelve noon couldn't arrive fast enough.

Agnes knew with the queue at the water pump and the big job of scrubbing the bucket spotlessly clean, Ruby would be away at least an hour.

Ruby followed her normal routine. Down the stairs, dump the contents in the gutter, miss the foul puddles, join the long queue at the water pump.

Agnes knew the young girl wouldn't see the front of the tenement from where she stood at the pump. There would be too many tall people blocking the view. If she could have seen beyond the throng, she would have seen a fine cab draw up to the door of the squalid building in which she lived. A woman and child would scurry across the road lifting their skirts and petticoats as high as they could, desperate to keep them out of the filth. She would have seen the driver-assist them into the cab, and the woman pull down the blinds immediately on entering it.

There were about four people ahead of her in the queue, and she shivered as she waited. Luckily it wasn't raining, but the ever-present black clouds were overhead, and the gloom was overbearing. She rinsed out the bucket with her hands, filled it halfway with water and went and stood near the privies while she scrubbed it with carbolic soap and a steel brush. She was up to her elbows in stinking water, and her dress was getting wetter. *I'd better get this bucket clean, or else Aunt Agnes will whip me again.*

She went back to the queue for fresh water for rinsing. Ruby was tired now, and her normal energetic gait had changed into a slow trundle. She disobeyed Agnes's rule and dragged the slops bucket along behind her, the enamel scraping on the ground.

The street was bustling with traffic. It was the day horse dung was collected off the streets to sell to the tanners. Ruby crossed the road carefully. With her full concentration centred on dodging puddles, she didn't see old Mrs Black empty her bucket into the street from her second-floor room. From her position high above the road, she yelled for Ruby to mind out, as the brown liquid hurtled down towards her,

Ruby jumped backwards and was hit by a dirt cart. The horse thundered over her as she fell under its hooves. She could feel the powerful animal forcing her arm into an unnatural position as it lumbered over her. The cart followed, one of its huge wheels driving over her leg. Unaware of the collision as the cart rattled over the uneven cobbled road, the driver didn't stop or even look back.

Ruby lay dazed in a pool of filth. Her hair was sopping wet, and her dress ripped and ruined. Her arm was laying at an awkward angle, and she couldn't move her leg. Attempting to crawl to safety, she was thwarted as the pain overwhelmed her. She counted several men and women who simply stepped around her. Another cart drove by without stopping. Mrs Black was looking at her but made no effort to come down and assist. In fact, Ruby's bleary eyes could make out quite a lot of faces watching from the windows up above.

She didn't cry and scream or ask for aid. She lay silently. This child had self-reliance, not self-pity. She didn't beg for help; she knew she would have to help herself. She lay there in the dirt, for what felt like an age, considering her options, yet in reality, it was seconds. Moving from the street had to be her priority. Somehow she needed to turn onto her stomach, bear the pain and drag herself to the gutter, then she would send one of her small friends to fetch Agnes.

Constable McGregor was coming off the beat and heading to the police station via Style Street. He looked about him. The scuttlers, dressed in their flat caps and scarves, were working the street extorting money or favours as usual. Prostitutes, too beaten up to work in a 'respectable brothel', advertised their services from the kerb with a toothless smile—all were successful in securing business. Ragged, barefoot children were more prolific than rats. There was a scuffle breaking out between two drunken women about who got to the water pump first. A cart with a broken wheel was holding up the vehicles behind. If he wasn't mistaken, right in the middle of the road was a small broken and beaten child fighting to get up.

She had managed to struggle onto her right side by moving an inch at a time. From her uncomfortable position, she saw the legs of a bobby's uniform. In her little mind, it was like the appearance of an angel. McGregor moved towards the child, dodging the traffic as he went. He bent over the little thing. Two large eyes peered at him; fire and determination raged through them. Under all the dirt and damp, he could make out it was Ruby Alaniz.

"Och, Ruby. Ya poor wee lassie! How did this happen?" he enquired, the despair evident in his voice.

Constable McGregor assessed the dire situation. He was used to seeing intense hardship in the Meadow, but seeing the youngster suffer like this was hard on him. Lying in the filth, her hair matted, dress torn and limbs lying at odd angles, he was paralysed by indecision. Sensing he was wavering, Ruby took control.

"Pick me up!" she said commandingly. "And find a wheelbarrow."

McGregor was not used to taking orders from small children, but the plan made sense.

"Here, Pete!" he shouted to a match boy as he passed by, "Bring me over Neville's barrow, will ya? I need to get this lassie to the Police Station sharpish."

A crowd had gathered on the street, and the tenants were still watching the show from up high. Ruby thought they were like vultures, happy to circle around close by yet offer no assistance whatsoever.

McGregor and the match boy placed a battered and bruised Ruby into the barrow. Every bump was agony, but the child was stoic and didn't utter a sound for the five-minute journey to the police station. There was plenty of noise coming from Pete, who bellowed for people to get out of the way as they dragged Ruby along.

6

THE FIRST HOTEL BATH

In the meantime, Agnes and Bianca had reached the Grand. Bianca was dazzled. Everything shone. It was spotlessly clean. There were bright lights everywhere. Flowers adorned the reception, and large gold crystal chandeliers hung from the vaulted ceiling. Her feet sank into the soft, thick carpet. In an instant, it made her feel that heaven was meeting earth.

Diego had been waiting in the reception area. He looked grave but smiled when he bent down to pick up Bianca. Despite doing the best they could with their appearance, Agnes and the child stank. All the eyes in the foyer gazed upon them.

"Let me take you to the suite where you will be staying," he said to Agnes. "There is a bath and a water closet. If you need assistance, the maid will help you. I have requested new clothes and shoes for you, the seamstress and merchant will be here at three o'clock to measure you. You'd best be quick you."

He scooped his daughter into his arms and called the lift. Agnes followed.

"How are you today, little Bianca?"

"I am well, Sir," she answered.

"You can call me 'Papi'," smiled Diego.

With her in his arms, he was close enough to see her hair teeming with lice as he led them into their suite.

"You are a princess now," he whispered in Bianca's ear.

Agnes looked around the rooms. The floral curtains were cotton sateen, and the velvet chairs were sumptuous. The four-poster beds were carved from the most beautiful deep, rich mahogany. They had brocade eiderdowns with matching hangings. Plenty of plump, plush pillows and cushions completed the ensemble. More chandeliers graced the ceiling of their suite. There was a tray of food and some fruits that neither Agnes nor Bianca could identify.

The maid watched the two ragged guests from her station next to the door. She put her nose in the air. *I bet*

they are scum from the Meadow by the looks of 'em. 'Ow,
can they live like that?

"Please wash the child's hair with paraffin. I am
sure you know why," he said quietly to the maid.
"Ensure that they both bathe properly."

The maid washed the girl as instructed. Bianca had
never been fully submerged in water before, and she
giggled and splashed with glee. The dirt under her nails
was removed, and they were clipped into shape.
Bianca's hair, once washed, was the most beautiful
white-blonde hair. The child was delightful, and the
maid soon softened her attitude.

"It is so warm." cooed Bianca, waving her hands in
the water as she stared at them.

"It is that. 'Ave you ever been in a big bath like
this?" asked the maid.

"No! I so wish that my Ruby could be here. She
would love this. I know she would."

"Oh. Now, who is Ruby? Your friend?"

"No, Ma'am. She is my twin sister."

Agnes heard the conversation and dashed into the
room, promptly calling the maid aside.

"Little Bianca is so lonely," whispered Agnes
conspiratorially. "She longs for a sister and has

made one up. We don't encourage it, of course, but she still mentions her."

The maid smiled and nodded discreetly.

"Of course, Ma'am, I understand."

Nevertheless, she had enough nous to sense the shifty aunt was up to something. *The question is, what?*

The rest of the day was like a fairy tale. Once cleaned up, wearing elegant hotel gowns, they were measured up for their bespoke dresses. The seamstresses also brought some off the peg garments so they could go out and pick up some essentials for their new life.

Agnes chose clothing for her and Bianca. Dresses, petticoats, sleeping clothes, coats and shoes. Diego insisted they take more than they needed. Agnes couldn't believe that she was never returning to Angel Meadow. Bianca couldn't believe the amount of food she could eat. Agnes had to reprimand her for putting food into her pockets.

Things were much less idyllic for Ruby, laying on a large desk at the police station until the boneshaker of an ambulance arrived. The vehicle was a simple basket on wheels with some straps to secure the patient. It had some sort of cover above the head to protect one from the rain, but its solid chassis and iron wheels provided no suspension, and it was as uncomfortable as the barrow.

McGregor and his colleagues lifted the child up into the ambulance as gently as they could, trying not to move the broken limbs. In agony, Ruby ground her teeth and clenched her fists, but she wouldn't cry. McGregor never took his eyes off little Ruby as he accompanied her to the hospital. He offered her encouragement over the rough terrain.

There were so many down-at-heel children in Angel Meadow, but his instinct told him that Ruby's extreme resilience would serve her well. He made a promise to himself that he would always keep a watch over her. *She's a fighter, and I like fighters.*

"Where should we take her?" the ambulance man asked McGregor.

"Can we take her to the workhouse infirmary? It's the nearest," he suggested.

"No," said an emphatic Ruby. "I am not an orphan, and I am not poor. I live with my aunt and my sister in Angel Meadow. I am not going to the workhouse."

"Well, you heard the lass," he said to the man, "she will not be going there."

"Since when do we take orders from a bloody five-year-old, Constable?"

"Mind your manners, chap. This is Ruby Alaniz, she knows what she wants, and I agree with her."

"Where are we taking her then, prithee?" asked the man

"Manchester Royal Infirmary."

"That's bloody miles away!"

"You have your orders, man. No more arguing with me."

McGregor knew that thanks to all the philanthropic money that had flowed in of late, she would at least be seen.

Agnes and Bianca were served dinner in the suite, and they dined like queens at Diego's expense. Afterwards, it was a pleasure to eventually lay their heads down on a crisp cotton pillowcase, in between freshly pressed sheets covered by the sumptuous eiderdown.

"Where is Ruby, Aunt Agnes?"

Bianca was desperately tearful. Her sister wasn't with her, and she hated sharing with someone else. Agnes had anticipated the question and had already rehearsed the perfect answer.

"Ruby has gone to the angels," replied Agnes with earnest, trying to make the news sound plausible.

Bianca looked at her with huge red-rimmed eyes. A fresh set of teardrops were forming, poised to drip down her cheeks.

"So, has Ruby gone to be with Ma?" the puzzled child enquired.

"Yes, dear."

"But when did she go?" Bianca insisted.

"This morning, while you were dozing," snapped an irritated Agnes, keen to close the line of questioning down. "Get used to it. Go to sleep, Bianca. Ruby is with mummy, and if you ever speak about your sister again, a big bad monster is going to hurt her—and then he's coming for you."

Agnes switched off the lamp and turned her back on Bianca in temper. In the darkness, Bianca was bereft. Tears streamed down her little face, and she wiped her eyes with the back of her hand. *Aunt Agnes had better not catch me crying, or something terrible will happen to Ruby.*

16

THE FRIENDSHIP IN
THE INFIRMARY

Constable McGregor left Ruby at the Manchester Royal Infirmary. There was no more that he could do for her, but he left his name and asked them to contact the station if she needed anything. It would be easier than trying to find Agnes.

Ruby lay down on a gurney waiting for her turn to see a nurse. The ceiling was ornate, but the room was draughty and cold, and it highlighted her sense of isolation. She was still covered with the wet slop from the street, and she stank. Ruby was chilled to the marrow, and her body was beginning to shiver uncontrollably. The movements made her arm ache. Thankfully, she still couldn't feel her mangled leg. She hadn't eaten or drunk anything all day. Her stomach growled menacingly.

There were a lot of people moving around her. The hospital was chaotic. As they walked by, they would push the gurney this way and that to clear a pathway. A weakened Ruby was beginning to feel seasick with the motion.

Eventually, a nurse got to her. She was dressed in a white uniform, but it was filthy.

"What happened to you?" the nurse asked briskly.

"I was run over by a horse and cart."

"Can you move?"

"Not really."

"What is hurting?"

"My arm and leg."

The nurse ran a hand along the girl's limbs and felt there was extensive damage.

"Orderly," yelled the nurse, "take this child to the emergency ward and get her cleaned up."

The orderly dawdled over to her. Ruby could smell the alcohol on him, and he had a cigarette hanging out of his mouth.

Ruby was wheeled down several corridors until she was dropped off in another big room. Later, she would learn this was called a ward. There were six low-hanging lights, only four of the lights were operational. There were about twenty people in the room waiting to be examined. A very young nurse came over to her. She was not more than eighteen. She smiled at Ruby. It was the first friendly face she had seen since Constable McGregor had found her some time ago now.

"We'll get you all cleaned up, don't you worry, young Miss," she smiled.

In full view of the entire room, she cut off Ruby's clothes. She washed her and rolled her onto a clean blanket. Then she rinsed out her hair, doing what she could to rid it of lice. Although grateful for the assistance, Ruby found the entire experience an utter humiliation. Being naked in public felt such an injustice. She was angry at her helplessness and immobility. Her despair was tempered a little now she felt less cold, cocooned in the bed.

"Can I get you a tea to warm you up?" asked the nurse.

It was an unusual gesture of kindness, but she felt sorry for the bewildered little child. Usually, children in Ruby's condition would be screaming their heads off by now, but she was quiet and well mannered, despite being on considerable pain.

"Please," answered Ruby politely.

The nurse returned with an enamel mug, with little trails of steam rising from it. Ruby took a few gulps. Instantly, it warmed the cockles of her heavy little heart.

Better still, the nurse surprised her by putting in a spoonful of sugar.

The bunch of twenty people needing attention grew to a crowd of fifty within an hour. Her gurney was placed next to one of the benches along the wall. The walking wounded waited their turn on the hard, wooden slats. Later, she was hemmed in position as another trolley was wheeled in tightly on the opposite side.

Her neighbour was a rough-looking boy, aged about thirteen. His hair, unruly, curly and red, protruded from beneath his battered flat cap. She stared at him for a long time, counting his freckles as a welcome distraction, but gave up—there were just too many. He had a blood-soaked bandage wrapped around his hand, which he was squeezing tightly to stem the flow of blood. He had been given strict instruction not to let it drip onto the floor. It was so dirty, Ruby wondered if anyone would notice a few more splotches.

A woozy Jimmy Townsend was looking around him, trying to make sense of his surroundings. The ward smacked of misery. The audible suffering of humans harmonised into a continuous low hub-bub of moaning, punctuated with the occasional high-pitched shriek of great agony.

A glassy-eyed boy lay limp in his mother's arms, eventually dropping his little eyelids and dying in front of everybody. The new mothers were traumatised. Those with experience were not. They were usually pregnant with their next child, their last one barely cold in the ground.

The usual drunken rabble-rousers were fighting to be seen before anyone else, causing as much commotion as the insane. It was hard for a layperson to tell them apart.

There were two lunatics in the ward. One was constrained in a dusty white straight jacket, fighting with the fabric, and trying to escape the shackles as he screamed. The other was a young woman who was half-clothed. She was chained by the wrist to a pipe in the far corner of the room. She was more docile but still a deeply disturbed person. Sat in silence, her inner demons caused her to rip at her clothes with her one free hand. Nobody thought of placing a screen around her to preserve her dignity. Quickly she became a source of entertainment for the lewd gaggle of men surrounding her.

Traces of human waste were smeared over the floor, with no promise of being removed any time soon. Vomit, blood and excrement-stained clothing, both for the patients and the staff, added to the sense of depravity. The amputated leg of some poor soul was on display outside the operating area for all to see. There were already flies sitting on it, a promise of the maggots to come.

The room was enough to drive anybody to madness. Jimmy looked around for something more cheerful to focus on. He spotted little Ruby. A nurse came up to her and smiled.

Ruby was tired and in pain. Her leg had finally come back to life and was excruciating. The agony in her arm was no better.

Both limbs were swollen to three times their standard size. Bruising had set in, and she was tinged with mottled blue and purple. Her mouth was dry, and her tired eyes were glazed. If it were not for the pain, she would have fallen asleep.

"And what might your name be, petal?" asked the nurse loudly over the din.

"Ruby Alaniz."

"Is your mother with you?"

"No."

"Where is she then?" asked the nurse.

"She's dead," replied Ruby with clinical precision.

"And your father?"

"I haven't seen him for years. I think he's dead too. There is—"

She was cut off before she could say 'Aunt Agnes'. Ruby was at risk of becoming an orphan in the system, which was the worst thing that could have happened to her. No one would find any trace of Agnes if they called to their home.

Hearing the conversation and understanding the consequences, Jimmy piped up from his trolley.

"She is with me. I got this hand by saving her. She is my little cousin; my ma took her in."

Nurse Firth couldn't argue with that. So, the child did have relatives, meaning that she had somewhere to go other than the orphanage.

The nurse left the child and moved on to the next person.

"Why did you say that?" asked Ruby.

"You don't want to go to the orphanage, or the workhouse do you?" answered Jimmy

"No!" replied Ruby with indignation.

"Pleased to meet you, Miss. My name is Jimmy Townsend," he said, smiling as he thrust out a friendly hand, his good one of the two.

"My name is Ruby," she replied with a weak smile, in too much pain to move.

"Where do you come from?" he asked her kindly.

"Angel Meadow."

"Know it well. I live there too."

"Yeah, with my Aunt Agnes and sister, Bianca."

"Ruby—Bianca—you two have such strange names," commented Jimmy.

"Yes, my father is Spanish. When I said he was dead, we don't know for sure. But we do know his letters stopped some months after he left for the continent."

"A-ha!" laughed Jimmy. "So, you might not be an orphan after all? I'll fetch your aunt if you give me the address."

Ruby dictated the details. Somehow she felt that she could trust him.

"I am going to fetch you another tea, and then I am going to give you one of my special barley sugar sweets."

Neither of them could know that this was the beginning of a friendship that would stretch before them for many years to come.

17

THE YOUNG CASE STUDY

Jimmy gave Ruby the tea. It disappeared in seconds she was so parched. She had not the energy for the sweet.

"Are you in a lot of pain, Ruby?" asked another nurse, with a tender bedside manner.

"Yes, I am Ma'am. My arm and leg hurt like anything."

"I am going to give you a few drops of medicine that will make you feel much better. It doesn't taste as nice as that nice barley sugar you've got there, mind."

The nurse had a brown medicine bottle in her hand. She carefully emptied three drops of morphine into a metal spoon. Ruby took it in without complaining. It tasted dreadful, but she didn't care. An overwhelming calm washed over her, and the pain miraculously drifted far away.

Within a few minutes, she slipped into a dreamless, pain-free sleep.

When Ruby came to, as she lifted her heavy eyelids, she could make out the dark outlines of three men looking at her. They didn't acknowledge her in any way, she was just another case for the day, wheeled into the operating theatre for assessment.

"This patient is presenting a fractured right humerus and left tibia." replied a man from somewhere in the room.

"How severe?" asked the surgeon, Dr Leighton

"Both are severe, based on our initial assessment when she was admitted." came the answer.

A nurse had removed the blanket from Ruby, and she lay naked in front of the doctors. Her little body looked broken. It was covered with cuts and black bruises.

"We can probably set the leg in a brace and put her in traction," said the surgeon.

After listening for a pulse in her lower arm with his stethoscope, his face became more serious.

"There is evidence of some tissue damage above the elbow. The blood supply is limited because of the awkward break. It's blocking the artery. We will need to amputate the arm, no doubt. As for the leg—"

Suddenly, Ruby was wide awake and fully conscious. She had heard that 'a' word before and it meant that they were going to cut her arm off. With all her might, she wriggled and clenched her stomach muscles and pulled herself into a sitting position.

"You will not cut off any of my arms and legs," she said.

The three doctors looked at her, dumbstruck.

"I need them," said Ruby.

There was no response. They didn't expect this small child to react to the conversation at all.

"You may die if we do not amputate," said Leighton.

"And I might die if you do," argued Ruby.

It was such an adult reply that the doctors stared at her in disbelief. Since when did an infant have an opinion and a credible one at that? She was so surprisingly commanding, so emphatic that they gave the suggestion serious consideration.

"Let us step away, gentlemen. I think it best."

The medical men retreated out of Ruby's earshot. The chaotic ward was still a cacophony of noise and flooded the whole floor of the admissions wing with shouting and hollering, so they didn't need to go far.

"Well, I never," said Leighton. "I have never heard of a child so firm."

"What are our options?" asked Dr Walsh. "Can we really save that mangled limb?"

"She will suffer a lot of pain whether it stays or is removed," advised Dr Roberts

"We'll need to give her a substantial amount of chloroform during the realignment or the amputation. It will be a risk to her tiny constitution. There is a good chance her little heart will stop when we get her settled on the table."

"Yes, that is a possibility. Then there's the risk of sepsis from the severing of so much limb tissue. We can isolate her during her initial recovery to reduce the possibility of infection." said Walsh. "It will be an interesting case study. It has to be said, preserving limbs is of great interest to our industrialist patrons."

But it was Dr Leighton who gave the final verdict.

"Let us try and save the limbs," he said. "Let us give her a chance. That child is a fighter. I have a firm belief that she has a chance to survive this. If her condition doesn't improve in a week or so, we can always amputate."

They went back to Ruby's bedside. The fire in her eyes sparkled as she waited for an update.

"What is your name, child?" asked the theatre nurse.

"Ruby!"

Dr Leighton, as the senior clinician, stepped forward and explained what would happen in the simplest terms he could manage.

"Well, Ruby, we are going to try and fix your arm, but your recovery will be harrowing, and you will need to stay in the hospital until your fractures have healed completely. At first, you will be kept on your own, in a room just off the orthopaedic ward to avoid infection from other patients. Your arm and leg will need traction, and you will spend a long time recovering if you want to keep them both. You do understand what we are telling you?"

The doctor was using very sophisticated language, most of which sailed right over her head. She did understand that she wanted to keep her arm and leg, and that was all she needed to express.

"I understand, Sir," she answered.

Dr Robertson explained that she would breathe in the chloroform and go to sleep. He couldn't quite fathom why he felt a need to communicate this to Ruby, mostly the doctors just got on with treating the screaming child. But perhaps that was just it. Ruby was not the average screaming child. She was bright. Even in her pain, she took command of herself, and she had an incredible command over people. She was not a prattler, so when she spoke, people were compelled to listen to her.

Ruby drifted in and out of consciousness where she would feel sharp tooth-grinding pain, worse than on the gurney. As soon as she moaned, her nose and mouth were covered by a wet rag, and she drifted off again. Eventually, she was mindful of being put on a cold, rattling metal trolley being wheeled along corridors for what seemed to last forever. She could only see the high arched ceilings similar to the ones in church drift past above her head.

They lifted her onto a bed, and this time the pain was so excruciating that she fainted. She came around with people slapping her face and putting some awful pungent smell underneath her nose. She was monitored for a few minutes as she seemed to stabilise. One arm and leg were in the air, hanging from chains. Once wheeled into position, she was left all alone in the room. She felt under the covers with her good hand and was pleased to discover she had been covered with some sort of loose gown to protect her modesty. After a quick glance around, by Angel Meadow standards, the place was reassuringly immaculate, much cleaner than the squalor of the admissions ward. The pain was unbearable at times, but a nurse who seemed to have a sixth-sense would appear from time to time and administer some more drops, and she drifted off.

Occasionally, a loud bell would ring. She would become accustomed to that bell over time. After it sounded, a cheerful face usually peeped around the door. *Who will it be this time?*

"Hello, Miss. Do you mind if I come in?"

"Hello—er—I am sorry. I remember your face, but your name has gone."

"That's alright, Miss Ruby, you were in quite a state when I told you. It's hardly a surprise to forget under those circumstances. I'm Jimmy. Jimmy Townsend. My ma sent you some vegetable broth."

Ruby was delighted, she had not eaten for hours and wondered if the hospital fed its patients. Jimmy's freckled hand took a white cloth cover off the bowl. It must have been hot when he set off, but now it was barely lukewarm. Ruby didn't care; she was famished. He fed her one spoonful at a time, and she finished it all.

"Is your tummy full now?" asked her kind new friend.

"Yes, thank you, Jimmy!" she answered with a big grin.

"You are going to feel right as rain in no time, you mark my words."

"Yes, I know," she said seriously. "I need to be back to health as soon as possible. Did you speak to Agnes and my sister and let them know where I am?"

Jimmy changed the subject, looking thoughtful.

"I am going to leave you these barley sweets now," he said, putting them in her hand, so she didn't have to stretch for them.

"Thank you. Now, tell me what Aunt Agnes said. When is she visiting?"

"Ruby—I went to the address you gave me in Angel Meadow. Your aunt and sister are not there anymore. The neighbours say that they left in a very fine-looking carriage and they've not been seen since. Do you know where they could have gone to? I might be able to get a message there?"

Ruby became genuinely flustered for the first time since her ordeal began. For now, it seemed she had been abandoned. *Where can they have gone? Could they really leave me behind? How will Bianca cope without me? And a fine carriage? How strange!*

"I don't know where they went," she replied, her confident mask slipping a little as uncertainty crept into her voice.

"You don't have to be afraid, Ruby," he said to her, "I'll look after you."

"I can look after myself!" answered Ruby with big, flashing eyes.

"I am sure that you can," laughed Jimmy, "but from time to time, everybody needs a little help. Especially now—"

He winked at her and pointed at her bound-up limbs to emphasise the fact. Ruby, for now at least, had to agree Jimmy's help was indeed a boon.

18

THE STEAMER TO MONTJUÏC

The following day, Diego's steamship sailed from Liverpool, with Agnes and Bianca on board, heading for Barcelona. The crossing would take five days if the wind and tide were with them.

The unseasonably harsh weather had whipped up a frightful storm in the Bay of Biscay. Waves crashed angrily against the portholes, then swept furiously over the deck. The ship was tossed up and down like a toy wooden boat.

It was too dangerous to be up top. Cooped up in the cabin, Agnes became frightfully seasick. Bianca, on the other hand, was having a sterling time. She was spending more and more time with her father on the bridge, fascinated by all the dials and switches. Diego gave her a chance to stand at the big wheel, and together they steered the ship. As he watched the child, he saw more and more of Grace in her. Her physical characteristics, the blonde hair and blue eyes, were obviously from her mother, but it was her joy and sweetness that reminded him most of his beloved late wife.

He felt a lump develop in his throat and tears sting his eyes. He stifled his emotion. After a cough and some furious blinking, in a commanding voice he said to his first mate:

"Watch the girl."

He stepped out onto the windswept deck. The challenging conditions didn't trouble him. He was an experienced man of the sea.

A gloom settled over him that not even the child could extinguish. He spent considerable time watching the ocean, the mistress he had recently regained in his life, looking for the answer amongst the white crests of the waves in the dark water below. Stormy weather like this made the contrast of the light Grace brought into his lonely life all the more pronounced and special. Clutching the railings to steady himself, he remembered the idyllic white little cottage they rented for their honeymoon. Then he remembered the hasty goodbye and the unshakeable guilt of leaving her in that godforsaken slum. *Why didn't I take her with me? Surely one more day wouldn't have mattered. I was already late.* It was a nightmare of guilt like a noose about his neck.

He stared at the turbulent water. If he jumped in fully clothed, its power would soon exhaust him, and then he would pass into the endless oblivion of nothingness, a serene end to the unbearable pain. So dark were his thoughts, even his little daughter could not show him a path to inner peace.

"Captain—Captain!"

The voice didn't know it, but it had just rescued him from a terrible fate.

"We are ten miles from the harbour. We are fighting a sixty-foot swell. The strong current is pushing us forward at thirty knots an hour. We need your experienced hands below deck, Captain."

Diego let go of the freezing wet rail and made his way to the bridge. The impending crisis cleared his mind, and he sprang into action.

"Someone take the child to her cabin," he commanded.

He sent a morse code message to the harbourmaster to alert him about their impending arrival.

"Switch off the engines, we don't want to overshoot the harbour. The current can carry us in. Reverse the turbines quarter of a mile from the wall, we will meet the tug."

"Aye! Aye! Captain!" replied the crew on the bridge. With his many years of experience, they never had reason to question Diego's leadership.

He left the bridge and made his way down to Agnes's cabin. He knocked loudly to be heard above the tumultuous sea, loud and raging. Agnes was looking grim, indeed. A bucket was placed on her lap, and she was heaving into it. Bianca was playing with a doll that he had bought her in Liverpool.

"Have you eaten something, Agnes? I promise it helps."

She shook her head, unable to voice a reply as another wave of nausea hit her.

"I'll send someone with some dry biscuits. Please give them a try."

Agnes nodded her head in thanks, although there was no way she was going to eat one.

Diego watched Bianca with the doll.

"What is her name?" he whispered to her.

"Ruby, Papi," she whispered back. Agnes didn't hear, the roar of the ocean was too loud.

Diego stared at the dark eyes of the doll. They unsettled him.

"If you need somebody, ring the bell, Bianca. Don't go on deck for fresh air, it is perilous," warned Diego.

"Yes, Sir, I mean, Papi" replied the little girl, distracted by her doll which was filling the big space in her heart that the real Ruby used to occupy.

Once ashore, Agnes had made the decision that she would rather walk over broken glass than ever board a ship again. She looked miserable and drained when she stepped onto the wharf. Eduardo had to steady her, offering his hand as support.

"A day or two and you will be fine, Agnes. Diego will get his housekeeper Esmeralda to look after you." said a comforting Eduardo.

"Thank you," said Agnes, with all the charm she could muster.

Bianca delighted in the opportunity to be able to run around freely again after being confined to the steamer for almost a week.

"Come here, Bianca. Stay next to me!" scolded Agnes

"Allow her to run, Agnes, she won't get lost. Everybody knows me in the port. They will surely return her if they find her. She has been cooped up for so long."

Diego's carriage drove up the hill through streets lined with huge mansions, Agnes immediately felt better. The idea of living in one of these houses was a cheerful thought. *Who would have known that Grace's foolish little dalliance would lead me to this life of luxury?*

Her shrewd, self-interested mind allowed her to go a step further. *What if I could find a husband here? Surely there had to be eligible single men looking for wives?"* Her grasping, ruthless brain went to work trying to find a solution. One thing was for sure. She was never going to be poor again.

19

MEETING THE GARCIAS

Diego's villa was spectacular, nestled in beautiful woodland, near the summit of the majestic hill, Montjuïc. The views over Barcelona and the sea were stunning. The difference between this bright, picturesque Spanish setting and the permanent twilight gloom of the grimy slum could not be more pronounced.

Agnes and Bianca were welcomed like royalty as their coach pulled up to the entrance. The hospitality was vastly different from that of the English. Agnes had read about the life of the well-heeled in plenty of novels when she had visited the Temperance Hall library with her father, many years ago. The servants were warm and welcoming, eager to assist and provided bowls of tempting fruit and freshly-made lemonade.

It was lovely and sunny outside, and all the windows of the house had been thrown open. Sets of large double doors led onto the brilliant white balconies. Each one was adorned with large pots of colourful flowers, their pretty blooms tumbling out over the sides. Ornate wrought-iron balustrades decorated the perimeter.

The fresh sea breeze blew over the marble tiles throughout the property and cooled it, creating a blissful calm atmosphere which was a pleasure for Agnes after the horrors of the rough sea crossing.

Bianca was entranced by everything that she saw, but more so by the garden. She had never been exposed to such beauty. The grass lawn lay like velvet below her feet. The carefully managed landscape had leaves of every shape, flowers of every colour, and a fascinating array of beautiful birds twittering and flitting between the trees. Everything was a wonder for the young girl.

This was the magical fairyland that she had always told Ruby about. *Ruby.* Somebody watching would have seen the small child stop dead in the middle of the garden, lost in a world of her own, remembering her twin sister, with whom she had shared her little bed only a week ago.

Like all twins, Bianca felt in contact with her sister in her mind's eye. Over the coming days, she spoke to her, played with her, and showed her the wonders of the things she collected in the garden, and about the magnificence of the things that she had seen.

She had no doubt that Ruby could hear her, wherever she was, and she had no doubt that her twin would return to her one day.

While Agnes rested in her suite, Diego took Bianca for a walk to the large fountain in the garden. The pool was ankle-deep.

"May I put my feet in, S—," asked Bianca.

"—Papi," he corrected lovingly once more, then added with a smile, "of course, my dear."

He gently removed the child's shoes and socks. Her legs swung about in the water, sending splashes every-where. By the time Diego hauled her out, she was drenched from head to foot.

"Can Ruby come with us next time, Papi?" asked Bianca.

"Of course, she can," laughed Diego. Although your dolly might get a bit waterlogged.

Hearing all the frivolity, Agnes came to investigate.

"What on earth are you doing? Look at you."

The sunny weather had done nothing to melt Agnes's icy tone. Diego and Bianca giggled at her.

"This is the way we live in Spain, Agnes. You had better get used to it, or you will become very dull. Mediterranean life is a lot freer than grim old Victorian England."

"I see," she said, making a mental note to be more cheerful in future. I'll clearly have to be more accommodating to secure that dashing Spanish husband.

"Please be ready with Bianca at seven o'clock, Agnes. We are going to have dinner with Eduardo and his wife, Carmen, tonight," explained Diego.

"Seven o'clock is very late. Surely, Bianca should be in bed by then?"

"There is not a cloud in the sky, Agnes. The sun will be up for some time to come. We do not march to the tick-tock of the English clock here."

"Of course. As you wish. I'll be ready with Bianca," answered Agnes with a patronising smile.

It was a short journey to Eduardo's villa, which over-looked another stunning vista from Montjuïc. Carmen had prepared a welcoming ceremony that included the whole family. In her flamboyant Spanish manner, she welcomed Agnes and Bianca to their home.

The four Garcia boys were well-scrubbed and stood in a neat row, from youngest to oldest. They looked like little angels while they were being introduced. There were embraces and kisses on both cheeks. Agnes felt over-whelmed by the degree of physical contact. The austere British didn't behave in this salacious way.

Carmen took Bianca into her arms and cradled her.

"Oh, Bianca, you are a treasure to behold. I am Tia Carmen, and you can visit my home at any time. ¡Preciosa nino gracias a la Virgen!"

Agnes was taken aback by the loud and passionate woman, and that would have been the same if she could understand Spanish or not. She was beautiful, and her husband clearly adored her. Seeing her bewildered face, Carmen spoke directly to Agnes.

"Forgive my manners! I was praising the Blessed Virgin Mary for gracing us with the lovely Bianca Alaniz, such a beautiful girl."

She shouted to the boys:

"Lleva a Bianca contigo" and to Bianca, "Go play! They will look after you."

The house was full of life. The children went outside, eager to play in the garden.

"Don't worry, Agnes," reassured Carmen. "They will look after her. They are sensible boys. Well, the oldest one, he is sensible. The rest?" With a shrug and a smile, she put up her hands. "¡No los se! Not so much!"

Carmen took Agnes to the balcony where a long table was set with at least twenty chairs around it.

"Diego, "whispered Agnes, "will Bianca be safe?"

"Como una iglesia, "he answered her, "as a church, my dear, as a church!"

More guests arrived and eventually all the chairs were occupied. The gathering was much bigger than Agnes had anticipated. As more people came, more chairs were added.

It seemed to Agnes that Carmen's parents had arrived. Eduardo's followed swiftly after, accompanied by his sister Maria, and her son Pedro.

Carmen's mother went into the kitchen and brought out plates piled high with tasty tapas dishes. The wine was poured, and the conversation flowed growing louder and louder as the evening progressed.

After a few hours, Eduardo watched his friend tiring.

"Let us go and have a port and a cigar," he said to Diego, "we need to get away from this mob!"

They went to the humidifier where Eduardo kept his finest Cuban cigars and chose one each. Eduardo poured them each a considerable measure of port into garnet crystal glasses the same colour as the wine.

"I would have thought being reunited with the child would have cheered you up, Diego?"

The two men were as close as brothers and were comfortable discussing their innermost feelings with each other. They had been at sea, at war and in gaol together and there had been plenty of time to talk.

"I find it difficult to look at her, she reminds me of her mother, and it—saddens me. I had hoped Grace and I had merely lost contact because of the distance and the difficulty in sending and receiving messages. To find disease had robbed me of my darling wife was a terrible shock. I want to love Bianca, but I think it might take more time for the wounds of my grief to heal sufficiently," he explained.

Eduardo had no reply, and the two men sat in a comfortable silence, both deep in their own thoughts.

"Will Agnes stay with you?" asked Eduardo.

"She has to. She is the only person that the child knows. I hadn't planned it that way of course, but, needs must." replied Diego

"Yes, Carmen has already planned to help Agnes settle into Spanish life."

"Eduardo, I don't know if I'll ever love another woman. Grace had an innocence. She was not tainted by the world or made weary by it. She found joy in everything she saw. Her happiness was contagious. She would have loved these people, this family. And, you all would have loved her back."

Eduardo had no words of comfort.

"Bianca needs you, Diego. You have been blessed with a precious daughter. Put your energy into her. It will be rewarding. My sons mean everything to me. Who knows, perhaps Grace is looking down with joy at you as you care for your daughter? If she is, I am sure you will make her proud."

Diego gave a weak, polite smile.

"When I go to sleep, my head is filled with nightmares. I wake up in the middle of the night, and I feel like Grace is willing me back to Manchester. I have no clue why. I hate that place, Eduardo, I hate it. I always have, even more now its slums and squalor robbed me of my wife. I'll never go back!"

Diego was passionate and emphatic.

"How can I help you? Tell me."

"Nobody can help me. I need to live as a widower every day until the nightmare fades."

It was almost eleven o'clock and time to leave. Carmen was in a fluster, packing food so the guests could take delectable slices of cake home with them. She asked the boys to help, then wished she hadn't, as it was slowing the process down.

"Goodbye beautiful, Bianca," said Carmen kissing both the child's cheeks.

"Gracias," replied Bianca with confidence and perfect pronunciation.

"Si, angel," replied Carmen with a broad smile.

"She is almost a Spaniard," said Carmen when she kissed Diego goodbye.

Diego smiled. He felt lighter after his heart-to-heart confession to his friend, his problem halved. Bianca was going to speak Spanish soon enough, and she was clearly settling already. It was comforting that she wasn't going to remain a foreign little creature. He decided to be patient with her and himself.

"Thank you for the lovely evening," said a grateful Agnes.

Bianca had fallen asleep on Diego's lap. The excitement of meeting her new extended family had exhausted her.

"It is a pleasure. We Spanish love to entertain. Especially Carmen!" he smiled.

"Agnes, what can I do to help you adjust to Spanish life?"

She had been thinking about this very thing herself and already had an answer.

"Diego, I would appreciate it if you could find me a Spanish tutor. Perhaps you can teach me in the meantime?"

"Certainly, it is an excellent suggestion."

Agnes smiled.

20

THE THREAT OF THE ORPHANAGE

It took Ruby three months to recuperate after her surgeries. In that time, the nurses grew to like her as she was no trouble to them, apart from the endless questions. She was inquisitive about the proceedings in the hospital. She had regular visits from the surgeon and his colleagues as they wrote their detailed case study notes. Ruby was delighted to discover she would be featured in a medical journal. She told them she would feel like a music hall performer being mentioned in a newspaper write-up.

Jimmy kept to his word and visited her almost every day. He always came bearing a surprise, either an apple, a sweet or his mother's broth. Constable McGregor was also a regular. News had reached the Meadow's Police Station that Agnes Edwards had vanished and he suspected, despite her bravado, Ruby would have felt very isolated. As a man in uniform, and upstanding member of the community, he evoked respect from the staff. He ensured that Ruby got the best treatment. He always complimented the nurses for their diligence when he visited, which meant the bed she slept in was always kept clean.

As well as regaining her health, another miracle had happened on the orthopaedic ward. Ruby made friends with a young woman called Tess. Known as 'Miss Allen' when she worked at the Charter Street Ragged School, she was admitted with severe burns to her lower legs and feet. The handle on a rickety old tea urn had given way, and gallons of scalding hot water flooded out of it. At the start, she was in a lot of pain, but just like Ruby, it began to recede as it healed. The nurses had suggested Tess meet the youngster, mainly to shield themselves from the volley of endless questions from her.

The nurses were trained in the methods of sanitation and hygiene as practised by Florence Nightingale. It instilled hope in the patients and the doctors. The Florence Nightingale Oath was one that they took very seriously, and as dependable career nurses, they were tireless in their commitment to excellent standards of care. The initial admission to the hospital was still chaotic, more because of the behaviour of the rag-tag patients than the staff. Once triage was complete, the nursing care was extremely professional. With firm discipline and well-honed routines, the matrons ruled the wards with a rod of iron.

Tess was a godsend to Ruby. She offered her the greatest gift she would ever receive—a basic education. In the three months that Ruby was hospitalised, Tess taught Ruby to read, write and do simple arithmetic. Soon, her enquiring little mind was fed by every young person's book that she could manage to lay her hands on.

Tess sat doing her needlework beside her, so she was on hand to assist with the difficult words. Not only did it alleviate the boredom, but it gave Ruby a glimpse of the real world. Soon she became bored with fantasy stories and was more fascinated by the facts in books of faraway places. Africa, India and Arabia held her attention, so different from the environment around her. But mostly she wanted to see islands, with blue water, birds, and fish swimming in it.

Ruby's treatment, once complete, would mean an end to her bookish dreaming. Soon enough, she came down to earth with a bump as the ward sister did her morning rounds.

"Ruby, the doctors have reviewed your notes, and they all say that you are well enough to leave."

Ruby was stunned. The dread of returning to the lonely slum almost suffocated her.

"We want to send a message to your guardian to come and collect you," the nurse continued.

"But I don't have a mother. There is my Aunt Agnes and my sister Bianca, they look after me. They have gone somewhere, though, and we can't find them—yet. Constable McGre—"

"My dear without a guardian to care for you, you will end up on the street. We will have to arrange a place for you at an orphanage. The matter is settled. I'll have no more debate."

Ruby's eyes were wide with horror.

21

MA TOWNSEND TO THE RESCUE

Ruby stalled for time. A few hours was all she could hope for, whilst the parish guardians argued about whose responsibility she was.

Thankfully, Jimmy was due to visit in the afternoon, and she was extremely grateful that he did.

"They want to send me to an orphanage, Jimmy! They say they can force me into one because I can't find Agnes, and I have no adult relatives."

"Ruby, leave it to me. I'll never allow you to go into that place."

Jimmy brazenly walked to the nurse's station. He looked braver on his face than he felt in his gut. This would be a challenge, but he was sure that he could convince them to allow Ruby to leave with him.

"May I speak to Matron, please?" he asked politely.

The matron arrived with a very dour countenance. The woman was curt with him.

"How can I help you, Mr—?"

She looked Jimmy up and down to assess his reliability based on his appearance. He fidgeted, trying to look as reliable as possible. *This doesn't bode well. Back straight, Jimmy. Best foot forward.*

"Townsend, Ma'am. James Townsend. Pleased to meet you."

He gave his best trustworthy smile as he held out his hand. Matron was clearly not in the mood for the young ruffian's shenanigans and didn't reciprocate.

"Matron, little Ruby Alaniz down there is my cousin. She is due to be discharged today. I have instructions from my Ma to fetch her and take her back to our lodgings. My ma is her godmother now Miss Agnes has left the Meadow. Ma used to know her dear departed mother, Grace Alaniz, Edwards as was. God rest her soul."

"You have never mentioned that you are her cousin at any of your previous visits? It's all rather convenient, Master Townsend."

"I did tell Nurse Firth when she was first admitted, just after the surgeon fixed her arm and leg. I was here with a bad cut across my hand. I tried to free Ruby from under the cart—see."

He showed the scar on his palm, accompanied by a face so earnest and angelic that it seemed butter wouldn't melt in his mouth.

"Well, I shall have to check, of course."

An unconvinced Matron, thinking she was being spun a yarn, went to discuss the matter with Nurse Firth. Jimmy was grateful she was working the dayshift else his rescue ruse might have failed. He saw the nurse look at him, then nodded. Matron turned on her heels to return.

"Very well, she is permitted to leave with you."

Nurse Firth had watched Jimmy visit Ruby almost every day for months. Jimmy didn't have to pretend to be sincere. He was sincere, and Ruby would be safe as his ward.

Ruby was given a new dress for her departure—new for her at least. She didn't know it had been left behind earlier and ended up in lost property. A parent who had arrived with a sickly child with a change of clothes had left as a bereaved one, fleeing to the Weaver's to numb themselves with gin, forgetting their bag in the rush.

The nurses were sad to see the precocious little child leave. Despite her terrible injuries, she had flourished during her hospitalisation. She looked well, had gained weight, and there was a healthy glow about the face. The sparkling fire in her dark eyes had returned too.

Jimmy took her little hand.

"C'mon Ruby, I am going to take you to my ma, Ida."

Ida lived on Stock Street close to two factories. They lived on the first floor in one room with an alcove off to the side. The room contained a big dilapidated bed that Ida slept on and in the bay was a narrow mattress where Jimmy laid his head on the occasions that he was home. The furnishings were no better than any other slum house, but it was made homely by the soft glow of a coal stove, and there seemed to be a lot of food.

Ida was a big, cheerful woman with a broad smile.

"Hello, Ruby, love! I've heard a lot about you. It seems you made quite an impression on my Jimmy."

Ida's pleasantly warm greeting helped Ruby relax a little.

"Hello, Mrs Townsend" answered Ruby politely.

It felt strange, knowing Ida so well having heard Jimmy talk about her for months, yet it was the first time they had met in person.

"None of that 'Missus' stuff, Ruby, just call me Ida. Now Jimmy says you need a place to stay. You can sleep on the bed. Jimmy doesn't sleep here often, even though he visits a lot. Sometimes I have visitors. You can eat anything you like and make tea anytime you wish. The privy is out the back, put on your shoes if you go out there. It is wet, and it stinks."

"Yes, Ida," answered Ruby. "Must I do the laundry or empty the slops?"

"No slops here Ruby, we use the privy. You can help with the laundry; we can do it together. We can have a good old chinwag. Jimmy says you've been learning all sorts burying yourself in books. You can teach me some of that knowledge in that head of yours."

"How long am I going to be here?" asked Ruby?

"As long as it takes to find your Aunt Agnes," answered Ida. "We will set my boy that task."

Neither Ida nor Jimmy held out much hope of finding her.

"Ruby, is there anything you need?" asked Jimmy.

"Yes, please, Jimmy. Can you bring me a book to read?"

"I'll try to find one for you Ruby, promise. Might have to make do with a penny dreadful, mind."

"Ida, where does Jimmy go when he's not 'ere."

"He, er, works, Ruby. He does a lot of night jobs here and there. You don't need to worry. He's big and ugly enough to look after himself."

Ruby felt comfortable with Ida, but she also felt insecure. She had no idea how long she would stay here or where her next home would be. No one had seen Agnes since she vanished in the fine cab. Jimmy was still her closest ally, but she might not see him much, it seemed. Constable McGregor was the next person she knew best, but he was more of an acquaintance than a friend. Ida was added to her nice person list for giving her a home. She thought about Tess. *She was nice. It's a pity I probably won't see her anymore.*

"Ma, I am going out now, got some duckin' and divin' to do. See you girls later," said Jimmy with a wink. "Ruby, I'll bring you a book. You be a good girl now."

"Thanks, Jimmy. See you later." they chorused.

Although she looked quite clean still, Ida insisted that Ruby washed with hot water from the kettle. Not taking no for an answer, she poured the steaming liquid into an enamel bowl and gave Ruby a bar of pungent coal tar soap.

"And behind yer ears, young lady," she instructed. "And take some charcoal to your teeth while yer at it."

While Jimmy was out, Ruby climbed into his bed. It reminded her of the times alongside Bianca. For once in quite some time, she indulged herself and remembered her sister and the fantasy life that they created while lying under the blankets. Bianca was always better at making up stories than she was. Ruby knew the tales were make-believe, but they still had the power to elevate her into a happier world. They explored lands with pretty fairy godmothers and handsome princes that came to a girl's rescue. Skipping along magical woodland paths to their destination, they would always live happily ever after. She told herself one of Bianca's favourite stories while she dozed off. Dreaming of her twin, she had visions of her flowing ash blonde hair and blue eyes radiating light, bathed in perfect sunshine.

Jimmy reappeared a couple of hours later. He told his ma that he was starving hungry and dug into a potato stew that had some marrow bones in it. He washed it down with some tea.

"Ruby! I found a book for you!" he said, excitedly reaching into his jacket pocket. "It's not in the best condition, but all the pages are there. It's the best I could do for now." He added furtively. "The—er—temperance hall got a new copy for their library to replace this battered one."

Ruby's eyes lit up, and she smiled the broadest smile that Jimmy had ever wangled out of her.

"What is it called?" she asked.

"The Swiss Family Robinson. It is about a family who get stranded on an island," announced Jimmy with confidence. "The lady at the hall said it was a great adventure."

"Jimmy!" yelled Ida, "I thought you 'ad given up all that lying. Telling me it was from the 'all. You must think I was born yesterday! I've told you that you are going to gaol if you don't stop with this thieving, my lad."

"But, Ma!" retorted Jimmy, "The book's so old and battered. A widow woman was having a clear-out. She couldn't read and couldn't bear to look at it anymore now he's gone she told me! Made 'er sad, Ma."

"That's alright then," Ida answered, no longer sure what was fact and what was fiction. "So long as nobody got 'urt."

Jimmy stayed schtum.

Ruby wiped the book down and started reading. The words were difficult, but she sounded them out, and they began to make a little sense. She sometimes asked Ida what the longer words meant. Ida would explain to the best of her ability, but she had never been to school and was often stumped herself.

"Ruby, I need to tell you something," said Ida, as her ward's bedtime approached.

"Now, I want you to listen very carefully," she warned, suddenly seeming serious.

Jimmy leapt up like a shot and announced he was off out on an errand.

"I've 'eard this before, Ma."

Ruby put down the book and gave Ma Townsend her full attention.

"I have visitors later at night most days. Sometimes one. Sometimes two. Gentlemen callers. We'll be—talking about boring things. Let's make a secret little camp for you using Jimmy's bed. From now on, whenever you hear the knock like this, three times on the door, you must climb into bed and draw that curtain. You make yourself scarce in that there 'idey-'ole and never come out—or make a sound. Do you get my point, lassie? No matter what yer 'ear—never come out."

Ruby nodded her head, not quite sure what Ida meant.

"I'll make sure that it's warm where you sleep and that a thick blanket 'ides you. I'll give you a small lamp, and you can read all your books."

Whilst Ruby settled in, Ida had curtailed her nightly services for a couple of days, but financial pressures meant the hiatus couldn't last forever.

By now Jimmy had supplied ample reading material to keep Ruby busy for a month. *This is the best idea that Ida ever had. There is so much I can learn!*

Jimmy was not keen.

"You make sure you put that lamp off when you sleep and don't leave it near the curtain."

He called Ida to one side as Ruby made sure the lamp was safely positioned on a little shelf.

"Ma, you could stop all this, you know?"

"It's me pension, boy. I need something for when I cannot do it anymore."

"But Ma, I can look after you," objected Jimmy.

"Yes, Jimmy, you can look after me if you steal. I don't want you in gaol though, boy. It'd break my heart. With your father gone, you're the head of this household. Just be a good boy and stop arguing."

Her son stormed from the room, slamming the door behind him in a furious rage. He loved his mother, but he hated that she prostituted her body to earn a bob or two. Of course, she hated the men that used her, but it provided a slender, regular income, which kept the roof over their heads and food in their bellies, week after week. With Ruby staying with them, they would need more money. There was no way her work with the men could stop.

Jimmy preferred to sleep elsewhere at night to avoid them. Working was a cover story. 'Working' meant using his thieving skills to make enough money to cover a few nights at the doss house. *It's a pity I have nowhere to take Ruby. She shouldn't be there either.*

Sometimes, the men knocked loudly and made a lot of noise, Ruby assumed that they were drunk. Others knocked very softly and whispered, not wanting anybody to know that they were there. Some men stayed longer than others. Some men rushed in and out very quickly.

The visits were always started with the prefix:

"Just put the money in the teapot, me darlin'."

22

HIDING AND READING

After a week, Ruby was so accustomed to the routine that she hardly heard anything as she immersed herself in her reading at nights, which was a relief to Ma Townsend.

Ida and Ruby would walk to the market. None of the women were friendly towards Ida, most hurled verbal abuse. She would walk past them without responding. Here and there, they met a friendly face, but they were few and far between.

"Why are they so horrid to you?" Ruby asked Ida.

"Ah little Ruby, you do ask 'me serious questions lass. Let's get some sweet cocoa and a muffin. It will be our secret little treat for the evening. 'Ow's that sound?"

Ruby smiled. It sounded fabulous.

It was unusually hot that Saturday night, and the Angel Meadow residents were taking advantage of a break in the rain. In the courtyards, the grimy folk gathered together singing bawdy songs and dancing, knocking back gallons of booze. No one was getting up early for church in the morning. It was humid, and the stink was rising off the street with the heat, but no one cared; they were numbed to living in the filth with a mix of booze and snuffed out ambition.

The dense clouds above trapped the hot air. It mixed together with the fumes from the neighbouring mills, tanneries and foundries and the atmosphere was suffocating. The occasional dull street lamp lit up the drunken crowds gathering outside the pubs.

When they got back, Ida put out the stove and closed the window. It kept the noise and the stench out to a certain degree, although the heat became sweltering. Ida got changed into a tatty, light coloured nightgown.

The secret knock at the door was loud and aggressive. Panicked, the little girl dived behind the curtain, concealing herself in fear.

Ruby closed her eyes and put her head under her pillow. She was terrified. Tonight would not be a night where she could secretly read. Her instincts told her that this was not going to be an 'ordinary' visit.

Ida went to the door, her garish dressing gown, tied loosely about her voluptuous curves. The cheap, scratchy fabric made a loud, swishing noise as she walked.

"Come in," said Ida, not her usual breezy self.

"You took your time opening the door, sweetheart," said a posh-sounding man.

"I was just changing the sheets after the last visitor." Ida lied.

The man slammed the door behind him.

"Take that gown off, whore!" said the well-spoken voice.

Ruby heard the garish garment slide off Ida's flesh and land in folds on the floor

"How about something a little different tonight!" he said in an evil tone.

"What would that be, Sir?"

Ruby noticed Ida's voice had changed. She sounded threatened.

"Pull that curtain across and lie face down on the boy's bed!" growled the man.

Ida went into a panic. She knew that was Ruby's hiding place. There was no way that she could expose her to the awful events about to unfold.

"Hmmm, I have another plan, a much better plan for you tonight."

"What?" said the man lecherously

"Come with me. It will be worth it."

Ida managed to lure the gentleman caller from the curtain and over to her bed.

Whatever pain the posh man was inflicting upon her, Ida was still able to spur his passion on. She wanted him kept distracted, away from Ruby. Ida cried out frequently. She begged for mercy because he liked that. She begged for more, even though the thought sickened her. Whatever she said or did, he didn't stop. Anything she did seemed to make him more insistent. Under her pillow, all Ruby heard was Ida screaming, the man laughing and the repeated sound of the bed banging violently against the wall. Oh, and Ida's voice in her head: *No matter what you hear—never come out.*

23

THE BIRTHDAY PARTY

It was Bianca's tenth birthday. The weather was cold, but the sun was still bright. She was preparing for the forthcoming festivities and had chosen to wear a blue party dress with white lace and matching blue sandals. Papi had given her a special gift—a tiny gold wrist-watch. She felt very sophisticated, reading the time as much as she could.

"It is almost two o'clock," she said, looking at the silver hands on the elegant white face. "It is almost time to begin."

Carmen and Maria set the table with a host of delectable Spanish confectionery they had made themselves

Carmen's mother had spent days planning the cooking, bossing the servants about, getting everything 'just right'. Her father escaped to a seat on the balcony and puffed on his cigar as he hid behind his newspaper.

All of Bianca's friends were going to be there. Maria and her son were attending. So too was Carmen and Eduardo, with their four boys, who now had a little sister, Isabella. The dining room table was full of lovely flowers and decorations.

"Papi, Papi! Come see what Maria has given me."

"¡Si, si, Bianca! ¡Vengo ahora!" laughed Diego as he walked over.

Diego had grown to love his daughter. She was an endless delight to him. He had made peace that he would never be with Grace ever again, but he was grateful for his time with Bianca. The joyous child brought life into his home and love into his heart. She was flourishing. There were the horse rides they took together on Diego's significant estate as well as ballet and music lessons. She helped her father sail a small yacht around the coast. She was accomplished in painting and drawing, but her greatest talent was writing. Diego had employed a tutor qualified in languages, and Bianca took to her lessons effortlessly.

Agnes had transformed herself into a sophisticated lady. She had stifled the aloofness that the English were famous for, and crafted it into a presence that was feminine, demure and alluring. Soon, she was accompanying Diego to glamourous social occasions.

Often Diego would compare her natural chilly disposition to the warmth of Grace and Bianca. She had immaculate chiselled features and flawless pale skin, like the statue of a Greek or Roman goddess. Her smile was radiant when she chose to reveal it. Carmen Garcia still had her reservations about Agnes, who seemed more interested in herself than anyone else. She never took to her, and she made sure Agnes knew that.

"Carmen! Carmen!" Eduardo would say, "You do not know the woman or where she came from. She was very poor and had to fight to survive, with no one to rely on for years. That is bound to make her a little insular. She has had to learn the well-to-do ways of another country, and she is making good progress."

"Mami Mia, Eduardo, we were also poor once. That doesn't matter. I am telling you, there is something wrong with that woman. She cannot be trusted. She is shifty and doesn't look me in the eye. I know she has a secret, some selfish plot or plan, and Diego is too stupid to see it."

"I was hoping Agnes and Diego would marry," said Eduardo nonchalantly, knowing that Carmen would explode. Once in a while, he loved to tease her.

"Eduardo, I never want to hear those words in our house again. I was hoping that Diego would notice Maria. She would make such a good wife. She is beautiful and kind. She is one of us."

"Come to me, Carmen," he beckoned with his best come hither face. She walked to him, and he put his arms around her waist, then lowered his head to kiss the nape of her neck, his hot breath gently caressing her skin.

"I adore you," he whispered in her ear.

"I know that Eduardo, but if you ever make that suggestion to Diego I'll—"

He kissed her again, this time on the mouth.

"Be quiet!" he said with a smile. "You are too fierce!"

She laughed. She knew he loved her ferocity and he wouldn't have her any other way.

Maria sat on the balcony taking in the beautiful view. No matter how privileged she was, she was still awed by the beauty of the city below her. She was sipping her glass of red wine serenely amid the party chaos.

"Pedro," she called to her son, "please pour your Mami another glass of wine."

"Yes, Mami." answered the boy.

"No, No, Pedro, I shall pour for your delightful mother." Diego interrupted.

Agnes glared at him over her glass. Diego watched the boy. He was growing into a young man, good looking with dark blackish brown hair and brown eyes. He handed the wine to Maria.

"Gracias, Diego," she said, gazing into his eyes

Diego watched her. It was strange how she had always been like a little sister to him. He had never really looked at her as a woman. While he wasn't watching, Maria had become beautiful. She wasn't as curvaceous as Carmen, but she was lean and perfectly proportioned. She too had dark brown hair with saucer-like brown eyes and a broad mouth eager to laugh. She looked gorgeous in her deep red party dress, trimmed with black lace. He watched her interaction with Pedro. She was gentle and loving, but he knew not to push her too far.

Agnes sat in the chair next to Maria, demurely sipping her drink. Eduardo saw Diego's eyes flitting between the two women and walked over to him.

"And what is your conclusion, Señor Alaniz. Is it a difficult choice, my friend?" whispered Eduardo.

Diego laughed.

"I was hoping that you and Agnes would strike up a romance. She is beautiful, and she is already accompanying you to all the social functions. She seems most presentable. The whole of Barcelona is talking about her."

"Oh Eduardo, you are such a romantic."

"How old is that boy of yours now?" he asked, pointing to Eduardo's eldest son Juan.

"He is eighteen."

"Do you think he will go into our business?" asked Diego.

"I hope so, my friend, who else will eventually run the operation for us. Bianca is far too free a spirit. And a girl."

Diego laughed. Bianca, lovely as she was, didn't have the temperament to run an international company. She was far too bookish and lived for her writing.

"Thank goodness I have your sons to take over the business and dote after me in my old age, Eduardo."

The party was a success and ended late. On a wicker recliner on the veranda, Bianca was sleeping under a soft red blanket. Diego bundled her up and carried her gently to her bedroom. He took off her shoes and smoothed out the blanket over her.

"Ruby—" she mumbled in her sleep.

Diego looked around for the doll. He picked it up and tucked it under the blanket with her.

Diego went into his room and closed the heavy ebony door. He undressed and bathed. Ten years since the birth of his Bianca, he was still a good-looking man. Well built, strong and fit. One or two grey hairs were making an appearance around the temples, but it suited him. Carmen said it made him distinguished. He was quick to laugh these days, and life in the house was a welcome distraction from the problems to be tackled in the world of commerce.

There was a knock on the door.

"Come in" he ordered, expecting a servant to ask if he needed anything else before turning into bed.

The heavy dark door creaked opened slowly. As the opening widened, he could see Agnes, who entered quietly. She was wearing a light silk nightdress and gown. It clung to her figure, like the finest of gloves outlines a dainty hand. It was easy to make out what lay beneath.

"May I come in?" she asked softly.

"Of course," he answered, a little taken aback at her revealing attire, but secretly enjoying it.

"Did you enjoy the day?" Agnes asked sweetly.

She seems far less brusque and icy these days. Quite a change.

"Yes. And Bianca enjoyed her party tremendously."

"She is such a happy child, Diego. Thank goodness she has a Papi like you. I dread to think what life would have been like if she—we—were still stranded back in the Meadow."

Diego lay back on the bed, hands behind his head, enjoying the peace of the moment, pleased that he had done the right thing for his child and Grace's sister.

Agnes walked across to the bed and sat beside him. She touched his hand softly, hesitantly. His skin was much rougher than hers from his years of hard work at sea. He was also deliciously warm. Alive.

"Are you lonely, Diego?"

"Yes," he replied as his finger traced along the silk covering her shapely thigh.

"So am I," she answered.

Agnes slowly unbuttoned her nightdress, and as each fastening loosened, Diego felt more drawn into the moment. He was trapped like a spider in a web, and he liked it.

She slid her feet onto the bed and lay along beside him. He turned onto his side, resting his head on his hand so he could get a better look at her—all of her. Her body was captivating, her ivory skin so tempting. He slowly removed his clothes, with Agnes nervously helping. He softly lay his arm across her belly, and with the gentlest of pulls at her waist, he beckoned her on top of him. He was warm and passionate, capable of getting a reaction out of any woman—except Agnes. That evening, she would return to being as cold as ice.

Diego attributed it to nervousness about their first intimate encounter, but he had misread the situation. Agnes was delighted with the new development between them. Diego was handsome. But, that was not the purpose of the union. For her, it was purely status—and she was determined to oust her rival, Maria, and marry this man—for his money.

24

THE ANGER AT THE PASA DOBLE

"Mother!" yelled Carmen at the top of her voice, then waited for her to appear at the doorway. "If Diego is so blind that he cannot see what that woman is doing then he needs to be spoken to. I am going to tell Eduardo that he must do something."

"I agree," she answered. "Agnes has him bewitched. She is a heartless woman. I can see it in her eyes. And the way she addresses the servants when she thinks she is out of earshot. There is a foul air of selfish entitlement about her. She thinks of no one but herself, and she will break his heart. I know it in my bones. I'll speak to my son. Only Eduardo can knock some sense into his head. Mind you, I have no idea what his thoughts on the matter are. He has kept very tight-lipped about it. And about Maria."

"Eduardo and Juan will be back next week. Juan is learning to sail, and Eduardo refuses to allow him on the steamers alone."

"That boy is going to be a fine man, Carmen, I hope you are looking for a suitable wife for him."

"No, Mother, it doesn't work like that anymore. The children want to choose their own partners. It is not like in your day. They marry by following their hearts, not their parents' heads."

"But how does a child know who to marry?"

"Mother, if you chose for Eduardo, it would have been that fat girl from the bakery on Las Ramblas."

"What is wrong with a girl from a bakery?"

"No, no, no! Enough!" said a vexed Carmen, "I am going to lie down. You have given me a headache," and with that, she swept out of the room.

Keen to cement their physical relationship and turn it into a matrimonial one, Agnes visited Diego night after night. He was disgusted with himself. He didn't love her, but neither did he turn her away. He craved the warm flesh of a woman in his bed again. He wanted comfort and companionship. *How could I have allowed this carnal emptiness to develop with Agnes, of all women? I am plainly betraying Grace's memory. My sweet, gentle Grace, who should have been lying in my arms smiling at me, full of joy, not the Ice Queen. Then again, perhaps it would be good for Bianca if I married Agnes. She needs somebody to call Mami. But Agnes is still aloof by nature. What if she is putting on a show about her love for Bianca? If I am honest, my daughter does not seem too enamoured with her. In fact, Bianca seems happy to escape Agnes as much as possible these days. And this fixation with the doll, Ruby? Was it healthy for a ten-year-old child to be that obsessed? I want to ask Bianca about her toy but don't want to seem as if I am discouraging her vivid imagination. She loves her creative writing, and she seems to get some solace from it.*

A fortnight after Bianca's birthday, when Juan's educative sailing trip was complete, the two households met at Eduardo's villa for paella and sangria. It was a casual meal, and the conversation was loud and happy. Around the table, the boys were teasing the girls. Carmen was yelling at them to stop, and Eduardo had simply given up.

Agnes was seated next to Maria. The wine was flowing, and Juan fetched the family guitar.

"Father, please play us something," said Eduardo.

"Diego!" called Maria, "When did you last dance the pasa doble?"

"No! Maria, not tonight!" answered Diego, laughing loudly.

But a determined Maria was already striding over to Diego and dragging him to his feet, tugging wildly at his elbow:

"Come dance with me! Si, Si!" she pleaded.

Diego relented, and with a flourish, he spun her into his arms. He was quite the showman. Laughing as he threw his head back in delight, he pulled Maria firmly into his chest. They moved in perfect step while everybody clapped loudly to the rhythm of the lively music flowing from the acoustic guitar. He took command of her as a bullfighter took control of his cape. Effortlessly, she flowed about his body. The dance became more and more passionate culminating with his arms wrapped around her tenderly as he bent her over, holding her at a dramatic, low angle. Her leg sensually lifted and clasped behind his thigh. Agnes hoped that was only done to steady herself.

Diego helped a breathless Maria to her feet and gave a gentlemanly bow. She laughed with joyous sincerity and clapped her hands above her head with sheer delight. For a minute, his heart lurched. Her happy smile and spontaneity reminded him of Grace. He became quiet. Everybody thought he was shy, but it was sadness that had overtaken him.

It had been such a spectacle that no one had noticed Agnes's growing fury. Her face was bright red, thankfully masked by the darkness in the candlelit room. She was humiliated. Worst of all she couldn't better Maria's performance. She would never be able to imitate that amount of sensuality if she tried.

Later, back at Diego's villa, there was a knock on his door. He rolled his eyes. He knew Agnes would come in without his permission, so he said nothing.

She perched herself on his bed. Her usually loose and revealing gown was now twisted around her like a silk shield.

"You move very well, Diego," she said coolly. "Did you enjoy yourself?"

"Yes," he answered.

"Maria is an outstanding dancer."

"Yes, we begin to dance when we are twelve in Spain," he explained. "I would love Bianca to learn."

"We English find the frivolity rather vulgar," replied a dour Agnes.

"Then, I am happy that Bianca is becoming more Spanish as the days go by."

Sensing the frostiness in the air, Agnes wanted to retire to her own room that night but stifled the feeling.

Back at their villa, Carmen snuggled up to Eduardo, resting her hand on his chest, nuzzling her nose against his neck.

"Diego and Maria looked so passionate together."

"Mmm," responded a non-committal Eduardo, not wanting to get dragged into another one of her lengthy discussions about Diego's love life.

"They suit each other, a perfect pair. Si?"

He didn't reply.

"Maria is still young enough to give him another child. A brother or sister for little Bianca," she continued.

"¡Madre di Dios! She is my sister! I don't want those images in my head, Carmen!"

"But—"

"That's enough, Carmen! Give me some attention and stop worrying about Diego."

Carmen and Eduardo started laughing. She rolled over onto him, but they were laughing so much that the effort towards seduction was futile.

An icy Agnes shifted closer to Diego, aware that she dared not stir his wrath or dampen his mood. In future, she would just ensure that she looked so beautiful that he couldn't remove his eyes from her. She began to un-button his shirt. She would try a little harder to satisfy him tonight to make up for her jealousy.

"Do you need me?" Agnes asked softly, her mouth hovering fraction above his.

"Si," answered Diego, "We need to think about the future."

That was all that Agnes had been waiting to hear. She kissed him with a fierce determination and pushed her angular body closer to him. She hoped her movements didn't seem too mechanical, too perfunctory. To make sure, she closed her eyes and feigned satisfaction with a series of moans, and he looked up at her. She lowered her head, so her long blonde hair brushed sensually against his bare chest. It also covered her blank face. Throughout their intimate moment, Agnes was not ex-periencing physical ecstasy. No, any smiles were rooted in greed. *My plan is working.*

25

THE WELL-SPOKEN MAN RETURNS

The cruel, eloquent man continued to visit Ma Townsend. The sessions had become worse for Ruby to bear. Now she was thirteen, hiding behind the curtain in silence, engrossed in a book was no longer a distracting shield. She fully understood what was happening to Ida. The only option for Ruby was to put her head under her pillow and put rags in her ears to muffle the awful sounds. She had asked to go with Jimmy some evenings, but he fibbed once more about working nights at a warehouse down by Victoria railway station, and 'couldn't help'.

With some subtle detective work, Ruby had found out that the man's name was Sir Rufus Spencer. He was a distinguished member of parliament, no less. Ruby had no concept of how the corrupt wheels of politics turned. All she knew was that people had warned her he was very powerful and could ruin her. He was, they said, best avoided. In Ida's lodgings, soon, there would be nowhere to hide. *It will surely only be a matter of time before I am discovered.* She worried about what would happen when Sir Rufus found out someone had been party to his clandestine visits to a common prostitute.

One day at the market, she asked Constable McGregor if he knew the odious fellow, and his reply was:

"Stay away from him, Ruby. He is an evil man who bribes the authorities to overlook his more 'questionable' actions. He thinks he is above the law because he is. Why does it matter? How do you know him?"

She didn't answer him, but the canny policeman knew that it could only be through Ida. Prostitution was legal, for the time being, as long as the woman didn't have venereal disease. He felt sorry for poor little Ruby, who lived cheek-and-jowl with the practice. He decided to keep a closer eye on her, in case she followed in Ida's footsteps.

He wished that he could rescue her from the mess, but nobody wanted a new mouth to feed, even if it came with free labour. Her only options were servitude or the workhouse. *God forbid that it would become the whorehouse.* His expression darkened at the thought.

Sunday nights became a regular appointment for Sir Rufus. Steaming drunk, he would stumble in. These days, three ominously slow, loud knocks announced his arrival, followed by the crunch of the door of her lodgings swinging violently back against its frame.

These days, Ida was terrified by his visits. She knew that she would be tortured until the early hours of the morning. Sir Rufus was a sadist. Ruby scrambled behind the curtain and into the bed. She crawled under the covers, squashed awkwardly in position to remain hidden. The smell of drink, stale cigar smoke and body odour permeated through the air.

That evening, Sir Rufus arrived in a particularly vicious mood. He pulled out a chair and sat down.

"Aaah, Ida! Come and sit by me." he sneered, feigning civility. "No, not on that chair, here on my lap."

Ruby heard his fat hands slap on his chubby thighs and shuddered.

"Now, I have heard that you have a lodger in the house," he whispered, barely containing his evil desire. "I believe she is young and budding, is that true?"

"I don't know who told you that, Sir. There is nobody 'ere. Tis just you and I. And my Jimmy-lad when he's 'ome."

He stood up abruptly, flinging her off his lap. She landed awkwardly in a heap on the floor. Keen to get an answer at any cost, he snatched at Ida's hair and yanked her head up off the floor.

"Tell me where she is, Ida, or I'll hurt you more than I usually do."

The sound of a gloved hand slapping across Ida's face rang out.

"There is no child here," she repeated in panic.

He pulled Ida to her feet and screamed:

"Don't lie to me, petal. You know that makes me angry."

She tried to say she was telling the truth, but instead, she let out a terrible groan as he punched her in the stomach with such force she went flying over the small dining table.

He started turning the entire room upside down, throwing furniture around, eventually ripping down the curtain against the alcove. It was then he saw the bed, the little lamp and books on the shelves. *No one lights an empty nook.*

He looked closer and thrust his hands onto the blankets. Feeling the distinctive lump of a body under the sheets, he flung them back and found the treasure he was seeking—Ruby. She looked up at him, fearing what was going to happen next.

"Leave her alone!" screamed Ida. "She is but a child."

"Oh, Ida" he answered her, "you know how fond I am of children."

Burning with lust, he reached down towards Ruby's heaving chest, almost touching her, but then pulling away, to save that little treat for later.

Instead, he grabbed the young girl by her hair and pulled her to her feet. She screamed for help, but Ide was still winded from the sucker punch. Abuse was so prolific in Angel Meadow; any screams were ignored by the neighbours. Ruby wanted to attack Sir Rufus, but he kept her at a distance with his long arms, still holding her roughly by the hair. She kept swinging her arms and legs at him, trying to hurt him back, but it was useless.

"Well, she's a lively little thing, Ida, I must say!"

Ida was back on her feet now and wanting to attack the evil man with all her might. She grabbed a long rag, whipped it over his head and tried to choke him from behind, but he was stronger than her. He elbowed her in the belly with his free arm, turned and pushed her to the ground, viciously and repeatedly kicking her until she was unconscious.

He dragged his young, tempting prize towards the door.

"You are coming with me, my girl!"

Ruby didn't answer, and she didn't cry. She had receded back into her shell, that safe place where nobody could hurt her.

Her last glimpse of Ida was her lying on the floor, utterly unresponsive, blood all over her. She tried not to think about the happy, welcoming face that greeted her when Jimmy first brought her home from the infirmary.

Sir Rufus thrust Ruby into the cab so violently that she hit the door on the other side, the force of it winding her.

"What is your name," he said in a normal tone.

She didn't answer him.

"Answer me, or I'll cut out your tongue and feed it to the rats out there," he said, stroking her arm with his black-gloved hand, gently yet menacingly.

"Ruby," she replied, "My name is Ruby Alaniz, and one day I am going to kill you."

Dripping with condescension, he smiled at her.

"Oh, really?" he enquired. His hand shot across to her neck like a cobra strikes its prey.

His stout fingers began to squeeze her throat, so much so she couldn't breathe. She heard the blood pulse loudly in her ears. It was like the time back in hospital with the wet rag. Her vision blurred, and her eyelids fluttered down as she lost consciousness.

26

THE HOUSE BY THE DOCKS

Ruby only came around when the cab pulled up in front of a large neglected Georgian house near the docks. The cold breeze wafted in from the water's edge and through the open cab door. She was still shocked and dazed.

Sir Rufus got his henchman of a driver to lug Ruby out of the carriage by her arm. He lay her slim, limp body over his shoulder in a fireman's lift. With his shoulder pressing into her stomach and the blood rushing down into her brain, she felt nauseous and lightheaded. Too weak to fight, the cab driver looked down at her with a malevolent smile, then raised his eyes to wink at his employer.

Ruby sensed that these two men were not just violent, like many a ruffian in the Meadow, but were evil personified. They were definitely worse than the scuttlers and their petty turf wars, which were over in a flash. Sir Rufus had exacted years of brutal subjugation on Ida.

Ruby would have to find a way to survive without her help. Constable McGregor had warned Sir Rufus bribed his way to be above the law. There would be no protection for her if she spoke up about him. She still had things to do with her life. Ruby was going places, and nobody was going to kill her. Most of all, she had to find Bianca.

"Kitt!" shouted Sir Rufus. "Kitt! Come and see what I have found for us. She will surely be an asset to you after I have had her first."

Sir Rufus roughly pushed Ruby into a room that looked like a learned man's study. It had a massive desk to the one side and a low leather couch on the other. Cigar smoke added to the smell of old books.

Kitt smirked as he studied her from top to bottom, pawing at her shoulders and hair as he paced around her.

"And where did you find this one. She is a bit young, but we can wait. Or maybe not, they need a bit of education these slum girls, and we can do the teaching."

Both men were grinning now.

"What a marvellous discovery," chuckled Kitt lewdly. "She's a pretty one, alright. We are going to make a fortune out of her."

Ruby felt humiliated and angry. Physically, she would easily be overpowered. Worse, withdrawing and thinking happy thoughts might have been a distraction when cleaning the privy—they did not work against imminent carnal threats. Their leering unsettled her. Like a prize-fighting boxer in the ring, she did her best to stare them out with her dark eyes, filled with fire. *I'll use my thirteen years of slum-survival skills to endure this experience.*

"Tilly!" screamed the coarse Irishman. "Take this girl to the kitchen, and tell Cook to find her something to do. I don't want to see her loafing around."

Tilly appeared, dressed in a tightly-bound corset and very little else.

"Yes, Kitt," she answered mechanically. She had learned early on into her 'stay' at the brothel, it was best to be obedient.

She took Ruby's hand, which was now trembling with a mix of fear and anger, and led her to the scullery.

"We keep a kitchen and a bar. The gentlemen visitors like a little food with their entertainment. When we are not with them, we take it in turns to do the household chores."

She seems about twenty, but she looks old and exhausted! All used up, I suppose. Nevertheless, Tilly was a kind soul and had the energy to give Ruby some vital survival tips.

"Ruby, Cook, will look after you to the best of her ability, and the staff will protect you. They hate Kitt O'Connor. He is a monster and a bully. He and Sir Rufus make an ideal pair. Just keep out of the way, and we will do our best to help you."

"Thank you," said Ruby "What will I be expected to do?"

"Its best you don't know until you have to," tailed off a forlorn-looking Tilly.

Cook greeted her with a smile. She was a stout woman, with big rosy cheeks and a few teeth missing, but otherwise fit and healthy.

"Hello, Ruby, lass. Just call me Cook, everyone else does," she chirped. "Come with me. I'll introduce you to the others that work here. I expect Sir Rufus will be needing you, Tilly? I'll take over from here."

Tilly nodded and trudged back upstairs with melancholic obedience.

Ruby was introduced to the rest of the staff at the brothel. Maggie and Stella were the laundry maids, and they spent their days washing and ironing a mountain of bedsheets. Cyril was the odd-job man who repaired the items that the 'johns' destroyed in their drunken states. Jemima was a scullery maid, and Cook told Ruby that for most of the time she would be working with her. Gerhard was a huge German, a solid wall of a man, that made sure the behaviour of the ribald, drink-fuelled patrons didn't get out of hand. Ruby later learnt the Gerhard abhorred Kitt's brothel. He only stayed to protect the women from those who thought it acceptable to attack them.

"We are going to be your family now, Ruby. We will keep you as safe as we can. Once you're here, it's best not to try to escape." advised Cook as she passed her a stale biscuit.

27

LIFE BELOW STAIRS

"What do you think of my new find?" Sir Rufus asked Kitt O'Connor.

"You were fortunate to get her. She's so—," Kitt fought for the right word, "—unsullied."

"Yes, she was bunked up with Ida Townsend. Remember? That stroppy slapper who refused to work here a few years back?"

"Oh yes," chuckled Kitt wickedly. "Now, I remember her. Only a couple of teeth in her head, body all saggy. Not nice and smiley and taut like this new one."

"What are your plans with the girl?" Kitt asked Sir Rufus.

"She says her name is Ruby. What a lovely name for a scarlet woman." He laughed. "She says she is thirteen. How glorious a thought that is. Being more interested in books than men, I suspect she is still intact. All the sweeter, eh?"

"I suggest we advertise her in a gentleman's magazine. We can make quite a profit from that young body, especially for the first time."

"I shall have her first, and then we shall lie to all the punters who follow in my—footsteps," smirked Sir Rufus.

"Well then you need to put your money on the table for that privilege, Sir," said Kitt shrewdly.

"How much?"

"One hundred pounds—and you shall wait a year before you savour her. We need to be sure she's old enough. I don't want closing down."

Sir Rufus's jaw dropped.

"I brought her here, Kitt. I could have had my way with her in the cab earlier. I throttled her to subdue her, being a feisty thing. But I knew the little filly would be a good earner for you in the long term. There are a good few years in her before she starts to fade like Tilly."

"Fifty pounds now and fifty upon delivery," said Kitt. "And you know that I'll keep her in pristine condition for another year if you can wait it out.

Taking advantage of a thirteen-year-old? Well, it might draw unwanted attention to our operation here. It will be a unique experience for you in these wanton times, Rufus, lying with a clean, unspoilt young thing like her. It will make your excitement—that anticipation of deflowering her—last a whole year. I think it's a bargain, Rufus, less than a shilling a day to secure such a treasure."

The thought was a tantalising one, and Sir Rufus was already getting hot under the collar at the prospect of what he would do to Ruby. This would definitely be something to look forward to.

Delighted inside, with butterflies in his fat stomach, Rufus carefully counted out fifty pounds, but still scowled has he did so in case Kitt decided to raise the price further.

Rufus had a mean mouth, a thin slit in his chubby face. His greying hair and beard were perfectly trimmed, the face of a typical aristocrat. His watery blue eyes stared at Kitt.

"When the time comes, she'd better be perfect, Kitt. You don't want to make an enemy of me."

Cook, overhearing the offer Kitt made Sir Rufus, had no idea where she could put Ruby that was out of harm's way. The patrons liked to wander all over the house, finding new places to fornicate with the girls. It kept things 'fresh'. She discussed the problem with Cyril.

> "We need a place to put the lass. If any of those lusty scoundrels come into the kitchen before Gerhard can catch them, she's in trouble. We need to set up a safe place for her. Longer term, it will be risky, of course, but we need to help her escape. She is too young for Sir Rufus, or anyone else."

> "There is a cupboard under the servants' staircase," said Cyril. I am sure, with a few modifications, we can create a refuge for her there."

The den had enough space for a few blankets on the floor, a lamp and some books. Ruby was reliving her years in Ida's house all over again. *When will the running and the hiding stop? When will I finally be safe? The last time I felt safe was recovering in hospital, and that was years ago. I hope Bianca is safe wherever she ended up.*

She realised that Sir Rufus and Kitt O'Connor were the hunters, and she was the prey. During the day she was relatively safe, but at night the brothel was as busy as a station. There were a lot of drunk men, and the prostitutes were no better. Sailors came up from the wharf, usually the roughest of the rough. By seven o'clock Ruby had to be in the cupboard in case a drunken loiterer saw her in the kitchen and tried to take advantage.

During the day she helped Jemima in the scullery. She was not allowed off the premises and Kitt made regular visits to ensure that his asset was still intact and had not run away. Only Kitt and Gerhard had keys to the numerous locks on the doors.

Kitt threatened his staff with torture if he found she was missing. They were terrified of him, but that didn't stop them from plotting her escape. Perhaps, they could get word to Constable McGregor to help them? Even if Sir Rufus's deep pockets were good at paying the coppers off, he was one of the good ones. It was worth the risk.

28

JIMMY TOWNSEND'S SHOCKING NEWS

Gerhard's conscience got the upper hand, and he managed to get word to Constable McGregor, who was horrified to hear of Ruby's internment at the O'Connor brothel. If a woman chose to be there, that was her decision. But imprisonment, well that was a different matter.

However, he could lay no charges because no evidence of a violation had occurred. If the boys in blue paid a visit, Kitt O'Connor would simply say that Ruby was a scullery maid and the staff would be too afraid to contradict him. The best he could do was tip off Jimmy Townsend to be his 'man on the inside'. He was a sneaky little snake, but could be trusted to keep a secret were Ruby was concerned.

Hearing on the grapevine where she was, Jimmy went to see her like a shot, pretending he was a delivery boy dropping off food. The reason for his visit would be two-fold. Ruby was amazed to see him in the scullery but didn't go over until Cook told her the coast was clear. As soon as she stood in front of him, she could see the anguish on his face. She wiped away a small tear that was dripping down his cheek.

"What is it, Jimmy, you can tell me? We're stuck together like glue us two, through thick and thin! It can't be that bad, can it?"

"It's Ma, Ruby—" struggled Jimmy. "—She's—dead!"

"Ida? But how?" she asked tearfully.

"I found 'er lying on the floor, severely beaten, by one of those bloody rogues who liked to take advantage of her. I only knew it was 'er cos of where I found 'er. She must have been there a couple of days. 'Er face was black, bloodied and swollen. I went back on Wednesday, and there she was. I don't want to talk about it. It was the worst thing I have ever seen. I'll live with the image for the rest of my life."

"Oh, Jimmy. Ida was so kind to me! I dunno what would 'ave 'appened if she 'adn't taken me in."

"I wish I could 'ave stayed when those fellas called round, but I couldn't. And I couldn't stop 'er earning a living that way either. Now I feel utterly responsible. Who would've clobbered 'er, Ruby? You saw and 'eard much more than me. Who would 'ave done this?"

"I can't help, Jimmy. I went for a walk down to the river on Sunday. Barely got out of the courtyard and I got coshed over the 'ead by one of O'Connor's brutes."

Ruby didn't give him a truthful answer. She knew it was Sir Rufus, but there was no concrete evidence. But more than that, if she told Jimmy, he would likely do something stupid in vengeful retribution and end up in gaol.

"Where was she buried?"

"In a pauper grave, up at St Michael's Flags, where else?"

It was said with such helpless resignation that it broke Ruby's heart. Ma Townsend, the kind woman who kept her out of the workhouse, would just be another person lost in a graveyard of thirty thousand.

"Thank you for telling me," said Ruby, squeezing his hands in hers. "You better go, Jimmy Townsend, before we are caught. Shoo! Shoo! All hell will break loose. Mr O'Connor is not a man to upset if you want to avoid a beating."

She hugged him tightly, then pushed him away towards the servant entrance to the mansion, as a sizeable lump formed in her throat.

Climbing into her cupboard that night, she had a heavy heart. She loved Ida, and Ida had loved her. With her limited resources and unconventional lifestyle, she had nurtured Ruby more than Agnes ever did. Ruby always had food, warmth and clean clothes. She was not treated as a mere skivvy, but a person, with an inquisitive mind, which Ida did her best to cultivate. Ida put up the curtain in front of the small alcove to keep her safe. That single bit of fabric had protected Ruby for many years.

Thinking about her old bed at Ida's, her thoughts moved to Bianca. Where *was she tonight? Who was looking after her? She must be petrified without me, with only Agnes for company. What if Agnes was neglecting her like she did me?*

At that moment, Ruby realised that life was simple. There were good people and bad people, and she was determined to be one of the good ones.

29

JUAN'S SHORT-LIVED PROMISE

Diego sat in the box at the Gran Teatre del Liceu, Barcelona's new and magnificent opera house. It was the place where anyone who was anyone would be seen. He was a commanding figure, and many of the society women in the neighbouring boxes were seizing the opportunity to watch the handsome Spaniard at close quarters. Beside him sat his English rose, Agnes. The gossips assumed correctly that there was some sort of physical relationship between them, but were mistaken that she was now the love of his life. Many were critical that he had not chosen a Spaniard as his companion, but criticism aside, they couldn't deny that Agnes was a beautiful catch and that they made a glamourous couple.

The stately Agnes was dressed in a silver dress, and she sparkled from head to toe. The low-cut tight-fitting bodice accentuated her porcelain-like décolletage and beautifully-shaped bosom. She was wearing an exquisite gold tiara in her hair and a diamond choker at her neck, a gift that Diego had given to his late mother, which became part of his inheritance on her recent passing.

Equally alluring, Carmen was in a figure-hugging white silk dress embroidered with seed pearls and diamanté crystals that accentuated her curves. She too wore a glittering tiara, a gift from Eduardo to celebrate the birth of their first daughter, the angelic Isabella. Her long white gloves stretched beyond her elbows, and on the ring finger over the glove was the largest emerald that Eduardo could find at Garrard's of Mayfair, the London jeweller to Queen Victoria herself.

Eduardo watched Carmen drinking a glass of champagne. Like it, she sparkled, and he couldn't take his eyes off his wife. For him, she was, without doubt, the most beautiful woman in the house.

Maria was dressed in a pure midnight blue dress with an emerald green bodice. The sleeves were off the shoulder. Her black hair was teased from her face, held in place with a delicate gold filigree circlet. The elegant coiffeur allowed Diego to study her beautiful face in profile. He was enchanted by the look of her, but there was something else, something intangible, that captivated him. She radiated a joyous warmth like the late afternoon sun, and secretly he liked to bask in her glow.

"Are you enjoying this?" Diego whispered to Eduardo with amusement.

"I have to keep Carmen happy," frowned Eduardo. "I would rather be watching a bullfight."

"I prefer the flamenco dancers at the tavernas to the opera," lamented Diego.

"But it is not too bad, I can spend the whole night watching the most beautiful woman in the room," smiled Eduardo.

"So can I," winked Diego, but he surprised himself—he was thinking about Maria, not Agnes.

Back at home, Carmen's father was looking after the children. Isabella was ten and Bianca was almost fourteen.

"Bianca, please read me one of your stories," said Isabella.

She loved it when anybody asked her to read them a tale, and she wasted no time in dashing to her room, then bringing down her leather-clad writing book.

The boys were playing billiards. They always fidgeted at the opera, so Carmen was glad when they offered to stay at home to look after Grandpa and the girls.

Juan was developing into a handsome youth, lighthearted, yet responsible—a lot like Eduardo. He had spent a lot of time on the steamers of late, and the more he was exposed to life at sea, the more man and less boy he became.

"I am just going to check on the girls," announced Juan. "Mama will kill me if something happens to them."

All his brothers laughed. He was telling the truth. Carmen still ruled the roost in the household even when she was on a night out.

He came into the sitting room to see the girls next to each other on the big leather couch. They were cuddled up, and Bianca was reading Isabella one of her epic tales.

He only caught the story part-way through, but what he heard intrigued him so much he quietly listened to the rest. He put his finger up against his lips, to reassure Bianca he would be as quiet as a mouse.

> "Ruby always looked after her twin sister Bonnie, especially when she was frightened... Her evil step-mother used to give Ruby lots of chores to do, just like Cinderella... One day, she was sent on a long and difficult quest... While she was gone, a prince came to the castle and took Bonnie and the step-mother to a faraway land... Poor Ruby was left all alone, and she was never seen or heard from again. The end."

Bianca closed the book and stroked the cover with a strange sense of duty and purpose. Juan broke his silence:

> "It's getting late, Isabella. Bedtime for you, Missy, I think."

Isabella's tired little face nodded, and she made her way wearily to her bedroom.

"That was an excellent story, Bianca. Lots of detail, I must say. Did you base it on a girl called Ruby, or make it up? I know you have your dolly of course, but I sense from your story you took inspiration from a real person?" queried Juan

"You've guessed correctly."

Bianca smiled, pleased that her story had made an impression, but a frown appeared soon after.

"Ruby was a big part of my life. It was a long time ago now, though. I have not seen her since I was four—when Papi brought us to Spain." said Bianca with far more emotion than was appropriate for the 'imaginary Ruby' Agnes always talked of.

Juan's curiosity was piqued. He had been wondering for quite some time about the elusive 'Ruby' character.

"Who was she? This Ruby? A friend?"

Over the years, Agnes's grip over Bianca was loosening. There were plenty of people to look after her since they left the slum, and tonight, finally, she felt she could take a risk. Telling Juan seemed the easiest option to test the response. She answered a little shyly, afraid that he wouldn't believe her, then rapidly gained confidence.

"Ruby is my sister—my twin sister. We're not identical, but we are twins, I promise. I think that's why our dear mother, Grace, died so young. Two babies at once were too much strain for her poor little body. Jenny Morris, who saw us be born once told me she was very petite and gentle, not feisty and independent like Aunt Agnes. For some reason, my aunt liked me, but not Ruby. They never gelled."

Juan gave her an encouraging smile, hoping she would share more of her intriguing story.

"I've had many years to recall the memories now. Some of them were locked in my stories, some locked in the recollections in my head. But this is not another one of my fairy tales. It is based on truth. I think it is time I share what I know. I want to find my precious Ruby. Agnes was beastly to my sister. I've seen animals treated better. I can't help but think she wanted her out of the way. Jenny said Ruby was named after a spectacular ruby ring my father gave my mother shortly after they married. I have no idea what happened to the ring? Perhaps Agnes pawned it to get some money. We were so poor back then."

Juan thought little Bianca had assessed the situation very well. The fact that Agnes never returned to Manchester with Diego tied in with the girl's story. If her aunt or Diego was spotted by the gossips, someone would bring the long-lost daughter over to them. On discovering she had deliberately concealed the second child, Diego would have cast her out of his home, and rightly so. There was no incentive for Agnes to tell the truth.

"But please, Juan nobody must find out about this. Agnes will explode. She can still make my life very difficult. If she knew how much I remember about Ruby, she would be incandescent. And you know how harsh she can be at times. But I can't help but think if she is alive, Ruby might need rescuing from a terrible fate. I think there is perhaps some truth in one twin, knowing what another one is thinking."

Juan looked on with an expression of disbelief, despite believing every word. Bianca told tales, yes, but not lies. She was one of the most genuine people the boy knew.

"You must not breathe a word of this, Juan. After all these years alone, I doubt my poor Ruby is still alive. I fear looking for her will only bring sadness. At the moment, I have uncertainty, and that gives hope. If I know for sure that she is no more, the pain will crush my heart to dust. Promise me, Juan. Promise you will keep my secret!"

She began to cry. Juan put his arm around her comfortingly and made the promise, knowing that soon, he would deliberately break it.

30

THE POORLY RECEIVED ANNOUNCEMENT

It had been an excellent but late night at the opera, and the weary adults returned home well past midnight.

"I am glad to see the house is still standing," laughed Eduardo.

"Standing? Standing?" Carmen threw her hands up in the air. "Just look at the mess!"

"But, Mama!" the boys all chimed in at once.

"Clean all this up before you go to bed. I shall come and check soon. Be quick! Scoot!"

As the eldest, Juan ensured his younger siblings tidied up and packed them off to bed. Then he went to sit with his father and mother, enjoying a nightcap out on the veranda. The conversation was in full swing when he arrived. Eduardo nodded that his eldest son could pull up a chair and join the lively throng.

"Agnes and I have been talking about getting engaged," said Diego casually.

Juan watched his father grip Carmen's hand as a silent gesture for her to be quiet. Maria didn't say a word. There was no reaction from anybody.

"Well, congratulations," said Eduardo, at last, desperate to break the awkward silence and avoid a row.

Carmen didn't say a word. She walked over to the decanter of cognac and topped up her glass. As her white dress floated, she looked like a heavenly angel, but under the calm veneer, she was furious with Eduardo. *How could he let this happen? How many times have I advised him that Maria was a far better suitor than Agnes?*

"Let's raise a glass to the pending engagement," said Eduardo, keen to end the awkward silence.

As they made a forced toast, Agnes smiled the most natural smile she was capable of and took Diego's arm. Everyone except Diego saw Agnes look Maria straight in the eye, sending the subliminal message that she had got her man.

As more yawns punctuated the conversation, they eventually wished each other goodnight. There was some tension in the air. Until the announcement, the evening had been pleasant, but Carmen felt Diego had ruined it completely.

Eduardo saw Diego, Agnes and Bianca to the front door and promised to see them soon to celebrate as they pulled away in their cab, then darted upstairs, exhausted after a long day.

Juan and Carmen slowly finished their drinks in silence on the balcony. Then instead of retiring to his own room, Juan followed his mother up the stairs to hers. Carmen was clearly irritated and snapped at him:

> "What do you want now, Juan? It's late. That news from Diego was so bad I have a headache. He has spoilt our whole night. What can he see in that woman? I had hoped when Bianca reached adulthood Diego would have paid for Agnes to return to England. It seems that there is more to their relationship than we feared."

> "Mama, I need to talk to you and Papa together, please."

> "Don't tell me you have also met a woman?"

Carmen threw her hands in the air and continued wafting towards her bedroom.

> "Oh, Mama, it's much worse than that," said Juan. He sounded so troubled that Carmen began to worry even more.

She stamped into the bedroom, Juan at her heels. Eduardo was trying to sleep, and was startled when she blurted out in temper:

"Juan has something urgent to tell us in private, and he says, thankfully, it is not about an unsuitable woman he wants to marry."

Eduardo raised an eyebrow.

"Come talk to me, son. Please relax, Carmen. Let's hear what our boy has to say, shall we?" insisted Eduardo, ever the voice of reason, and not in the mood for her fury before he retired for the night.

Juan divulged Bianca's promise.

"I swear Mama, I did not hear things. I am convinced there really is a Ruby, Bianca's twin. She said the girl was named after a ruby ring Diego gave to her mother. Do you remember him talking about such a gift, Papa? That would be some proof to support Bianca's theory. If Diego gave Grace a ruby ring—well—perhaps there really is something in it after all?" said Juan seriously.

Carmen exploded:

"Eduardo! Go to Diego! Now! Tell him. Enquire about the ring. He has a right to know if he has a second, long-lost daughter. This cannot be left until the morning! How could Agnes hate her own sister's flesh and blood so much? Abandon her in a slum of all places? I told you that woman was a menace. She is evil. Evil!"

Carmen all but dressed Eduardo and pushed him out of their bedroom. As his cab clattered along the cobbled hilltop road to Diego's villa, he was terrified about the pivotal conversation that awaited him. Apart from asking for Carmen's hand in marriage, he was sure he would never ever utter such important words again in his lifetime.

All the servants had retired for the night, and Diego had decided to have one last drink to reflect on the frosty reception he had got when he mentioned his impending engagement. *Do they know something I don't? Am I making a grave mistake with Agnes?* His thoughts were interrupted when Eduardo hammered on the door like a man possessed. Diego opened it, surprised to see his friend, wondering what all the commotion could be for. He thought he had realised and joked:

"Carmen must be furious with you if you are coming to sleep here! Did you finally confess to her that you loathe opera?" smiled Diego.

Eduardo's expression was serious. There was no smile in return. Diego knew his friend well enough to appreciate that something was indeed amiss. He opened the door wide and stood to one side.

"You'd better come in."

They walked to the sitting room, Diego leading, a nervous Eduardo following two paces behind.

Eduardo collapsed in a chair, the weight of the world clearly on his shoulders. Diego poured them each a brandy. It looked like they would need it. Wanting to second-guess what was upsetting his friend, Diego attempted to make sense of the situation.

"Why are you so serious? Are you here to tell me that one of our steamships has sunk in the recent storms?"

"No, Diego. It's not that my friend."

"Don't tell me, Carmen has sent you to complain about me wanting Agnes for my wife? Grace has been gone so long now! Am I not allowed to move on unless it's with Maria?"

"Diego, it is about something Bianca told Juan tonight. The news almost stopped my heart when he told me. I was shocked. I trust my boy, and I know that he would never misconstrue Bianca's words."

Eduardo repeated Juan's story.

"So, I must ask you, did you give Grace that ruby ring on your honeymoon."

Diego was transported to that moment and relived it in his head like it was yesterday.

"Well?" demanded his friend? "Did you? Tell me, man! Tell me."

Diego nodded in silence then took a big slug of brandy to try and slow his whirring brain. He didn't know what to say. The sense of betrayal in the air was palpable.

"That witch, letting me think I had one daughter when I have two. Who does she think she is? I have been such a fool, Eduardo, such a stupid, stupid fool. No wonder Bianca kept mentioning Ruby. The bond between twins is such a strong one. I have left another one of Grace's beautiful children to fend for herself in that godforsaken hole Manchester. What if—"

Diego felt the thought of considering what might have happened to Ruby was worse than knowing for sure. He sat, leaning forward in his chair, elbows on his knees and his hands running through his thick dark hair.

"I bought the ruby ring. It has to be true. Bianca wasn't even born when I gave it to Grace. She couldn't concoct a tale like this, even if she has a vivid imagination. There is truth in it. She has never stopped mentioning Ruby in all the time I have known her. And now, I know why!"

"You must speak to Agnes tomorrow. She is the only person who will know the truth. She is the only person who can solve the puzzle."

"No! I bought that ring, do you hear me!" snarled Diego doing his best not to shout, "I cannot wait until tomorrow, I am going to get the truth out of her now!"

Diego stood up to leave and begin his own Spanish Inquisition. At the same time Eduardo, now on tenterhooks, jumped to attention.

He rested his hand on his friend's shoulder and said softly:

"Let me know what Agnes says. You know where I am if you need me."

Understandably, Diego wasn't in the mood for pleasantries and swiftly bundled his friend outside and back to his cab. He thanked him once again for his information, then slid back into his villa, closing the door behind him.

31

THE LATE-NIGHT CONFRONTATION

Diego climbed his stairs two at a time. He stood in front of his bedroom door, hesitant, confused, knowing that Agnes was waiting for him under the covers.

Could Agnes really have betrayed my trust all these years? Could she really have been that self-serving? If so, what has she put Bianca through? What has she put Ruby through? How will I find her? The best and worst person to help him with what to do next was Agnes, and by God, she was going to tell him everything. The time for thinking was over. He tore through the door. Agnes was lying naked in his bed, ready to convince him of her undying love.

"Get up and get dressed," he ordered, throwing her dressing gown at her.

"Diego! What's happened?" she asked.

"Something terrible, Agnes. Eduardo has just alerted me."

"Is it one of the steamers? I hope not, I feel so ill-equipped to help you with your business affairs."

Agnes was slow to get out of bed.

"I told you to get up and get dressed—now!" Diego roared.

He didn't care if the whole of Barcelona heard him. He wanted answers. Speedily she put her gown on and sat on a chair, waiting for him to say what was wrong. He leaned over to her ear and said with a menacing tone:

"It's quite simple. I want you to tell me about Ruby."

Agnes played dumb to give her a few precious seconds to come up with a plan.

"Who?" she said, pretending to look perplexed as her mind worked overtime.

How had he found out? What on earth should I tell him? Stick to the good old story.

"Tell—me—about—Ruby!" He snarled again, not taking kindly to her delay in responding.

"Oh, Ruby! Yes. It was such a shame. Only Bianca survived." she lied.

"Grace gave birth to twins?"

"Yes. But the other child, the one she called Ruby, died within hours. I never wanted to tell you because I wanted to spare you the pain. Telling you wouldn't bring her back. Her grave was washed away like Grace's. You were so troubled back then, Diego. I thought it would break your heart all over again. You were devastated, remember? Grace would have been livid if she knew I caused you more, avoidable, upset."

Trying to deflect the damage, Agnes stroked the hand on her shoulder, put there to hold her in place during his interrogation.

"Bianca has been referring to Ruby as a living person for years. Are you telling me every instance was a figment of her imagination?"

"Yes.

"Did Bianca tell you all this when we got back to Eduardo's? You know that the child has a fanciful mind. She was telling Isabella stories all night."

"No. Bianca didn't tell me. I learned it from a very reliable source."

"Who?" she retaliated, her true colours starting to show through.

He was losing his patience now and grabbed her about the face, roughly squashing the flesh up against her cheekbones.

"What did you do with my child? She was young, just a few years old when you cruelly abandoned her. She—Ruby—survived birth. Stop lying to me." he insisted.

"I have already told you. She died. If there were two infants for me to look after, you would have needed me here all the more. If I was so desperate to flee Angel Meadow, why would I hide a child? Tell me! This is nonsense!"

Diego knew that she was lying to him. She knew far more than she was letting on. He looked at her and all the old feelings from the time of Grace's death came flooding back. Guilt, a paralysing sorrow, regret and fury at the cruel blow that had struck him. He was furious the woman he had shown considerable generosity to for over a decade wouldn't give him the information he wanted.

Now, Agnes's sole focus was saving her own skin.

"Diego, that is the past. It was a long time ago. We are to marry, and we need to look to the future."

"Where is my child, Agnes!" demanded Diego, his voice rising.

"Calm down. I told you. Come here, my love. I understand your sorrow."

She put out her arms to him, and he pushed them aside.

"Tell me where Ruby is," he screamed, shaking her by the shoulders.

Agnes tried to shrug off his grip, and the responsibility for the betrayal. She failed.

Diego had never struck a woman, but his reaction was a result of frustration and desperation. With a swift stinging slap across the face with his open palm, Agnes spun off the chair and landed on the ground.

Angrily, she turned to look at him. Her mouth and nose were bleeding. He was too angry to care.

"Where is she?"

Agnes looked up at him like the vicious cornered dog that she was.

"I left Ruby in Angel Meadow, and I hope that she is dead."

"Why, Agnes? Why did you leave her?"

"I hated her. Happy?"

"Why!" he bellowed!

She struggled to her feet and yelled back at him, her contorted face inches away from his.

"Because they were not my children. They were my dead sister's children, foisted upon me against my will. I didn't want either of them! But at least, if I kept one, I had a route out of the slum. We were heading for the workhouse, or St Michael's Flags, whichever happened first. You came along. I saw a chance, and I took it."

Diego left the room as Agnes wiped the blood off her face. He didn't want hitting her again on his conscience.

He made his way downstairs and roused his manservant.

"Take a message to Eduardo and be fast. Tell him that we are sailing for Manchester. Juan must have the ship ready to leave by five o'clock tomorrow afternoon."

"Anything else, Sir?"

"Yes," said Diego, "tell him that we are going to find Ruby."

Worried about their friend and unable to sleep, Eduardo and Carmen heard the clip-clop of hooves as Diego's valet arrived. They rushed to the door and opened it, then stood in silence, listening to the message.

"Tell Master Diego all will be ready for setting sail tomorrow from Barcelona."

Carmen did her best to be positive.

"Eduardo, Juan, you bring that girl home safely. She is one of ours. I'll light candles to the Virgin. Mama and I will go to mass twice a day. You will find Ruby alive. I know it, Eduardo. God will go with you."

32

THE ADVANCE
BOOKING FOR
SATURDAY NIGHT

Ruby turned fourteen on a miserable wet day. She spent the day scrubbing the kitchen floor and mangling yet more bedsheets.

Over the past few months, Ruby had developed into an exotic beauty. Black lashes framed her smoky eyes, eyes that glinted with passion, enhancing the perception that she could see into your very soul. Her smile was rare and shy, and showed a row of perfect teeth. She had lost the qualities of a girl and was beginning to display the physique of a young woman. Her tall, willowy frame had sensual curves, those irresistible curves that men would pay anything to touch.

Kitt O'Connor would allow anything in his brothel. It was its unique selling point amongst all the others in the

Manchester area. Unbeknownst to him, Gerhard the German giant, paced the hallways of the massive house not only to check that the dues were paid but to protect the ladies from violence. That spared them from the worst excesses of lust. If he discovered anything untoward, he would meet the perpetrator as they made their way home and persuade them that any further abuse could cost them an arm or a leg. There were very few arguments, and the men would either return with more respect or move on to a more lenient establishment.

This benevolent service endeared Gerhard to the ladies who offered to pay him in kind, the only currency they had unless a few coins fell out of a client's pocket and got lost in the bedclothes. The ill-tempered German would ignore them.

Kitt and Sir Rufus were having another Thursday meeting in his study, puffing away at thick, pungent cigars.

"I want to book a room with Ruby for Saturday night," said the politician. "It will be exclusive, of course. I have invited a few friends to join me."

"That is going to cost you extra, Sir Rufus."

"I have already put a lot of money on the table—one hundred pounds might I remind you." he griped, irritated that Kitt was trying to tap him up for even more money.

"Our arrangement was a fifty-pound deposit to keep her here until she was ripe and the final payment of fifty pounds on delivery. We did not factor in additional—spectators or participants." reminded Kitt O'Connor, looking him directly in the eye.

"I don't want to make things 'difficult' for your business" warned Sir Rufus, "but if you push me, I may have to."

Kitt didn't like being threatened.

"Business is business, Rufus. I can mention the girl's existence to a few wealthy fellows in the area, and I'll make more in one night than I can get from you."

Rufus gave a pinched look as Kitt laughed out loud before reassuring him.

"There's no need for such drastic measures. Your friends are welcome to observe at fifty pounds ahead. It is a bargain considering the tip-top condition that I have kept her in, so she's perfect for plucking."

"So be it. I paid for her upkeep with the deposit," growled Sir Rufus. "I want to see the goods—now."

"Of course," smiled Kitt. "Tilly!" he yelled at the top of his voice, "Bring Ruby here. Now!"

Ruby had a clear understanding of what happened upstairs. The kitchen staff made a point of never allowing her into the house without Gerhard close by her, and even then only during the day.

That dark, miserable afternoon, the staff were fighting against the stormy weather as they ran their errands over at the market. There was a lot of preparation to do for the evening. A large party had made a booking for meals and girls. Gerhard was in the stable outside pacifying the horses, startled by the thunder.

Tilly stuck her head around the cupboard door and said:

"Kitt wants to see you now, Ruby."

"Where is Gerhard?" she asked Cook.

"Tending the horses. It is bedlam out there."

Kitt's voice boomed down the stairwell.

"Tilly! Bring her now, before I punish the pair of you for your insolence!"

"I'll try and help if there is trouble. I think today is the day. Sir Rufus is in Kitt's office. It is not a good sign, I'm afraid, Ruby."

The skeleton kitchen staff stood around Tilly, taking it all in. Keeping young Ruby safe was their first priority. Everyone loathed the brute that was Sir Rufus.

Tilly took Ruby into the study.

"Mmm," said Sir Rufus licking his lips in anticipation of the treat to come. "You have developed into a delicious little something over the last year."

He ran the tip of his cane along the outside of Ruby's thigh, raising the hem of her dress almost up to her knee. Kit gave him a threatening look indicating that Rufus still owed him fifty pounds.

Desperately tempted to loosen her hair from its bun, he resisted. He murmured:

"It's no surprise to me. I saw the potential a long time ago."

Ruby was trembling inside but was determined not to show it. She had a moment when she almost spilt a tear, but willed herself out of it, imagining Sir Rufus's death. She had developed a few scenarios of his final moments which kept her motivated to stay alive and strong. After what he did to Ida, it was easy to focus on the evil in him, to remove any moral objections her brain might have had to her murderous fantasies.

"Come here!" he instructed Ruby.

She didn't move.

"I ordered you to come here!"

Once again, Ruby ignored his direction. Sir Rufus knew if he lost his temper, he would embarrass himself in front of Kitt, and he didn't want Gerhard sniffing around later when the time would come to experience the girl.

Instead, he took that one step nearer and began to stroke her hair, and she looked into his eyes.

> "I am going to watch you die," she whispered
> softly with an evil glint about her gaze.

Her confident, insolent challenge filled Sir Rufus with fury, and he could no longer contain himself. He grabbed her by the hair, spinning her around and pinning her to the wall. He began to pull up her dress and began to move his hand up her leg. She could smell his stale cigar and alcohol breath as he panted down her neck; the awful smell that had permeated Ida's flat while he was there. Even with the windows open, it took an age to dissipate.

> "Stop!" yelled Tilly! "You don't want to spoil all
> the fun demonstrating your prowess to your
> friends on Saturday night, do you? They will be
> expecting quite a show after all this preparation,
> Sir Rufus."

Appealing to his ego had worked. Thankfully, what Tilly said made sense and he let Ruby go.

> "Get her out of here. Now's not the time," he said
> with a wicked scowl.

Kitt was disappointed, he thought payday might come early. Tilly couldn't get Ruby out of the room fast enough. She practically dragged Ruby down the stairway and into the kitchen.

Ruby's entire body was shaking as she made her way to her sanctuary, the little secret cupboard. She climbed in and pulled the door closed behind her. Then she cried. She cried for Grace, Bianca, and the father she never knew. She cried for Ida. She unburdened every sorrow that she had experienced in the last fourteen years.

"We'd better come up with a plan, and soon!" Tilly hissed at Cook. "On Saturday night that monster and his friends are coming here for Ruby. Kitt wants to advertise her after that. He believes he will make a king's ransom out of her. He has put some of his henchmen at the back gate to make sure she can't escape. Be careful of them."

"We'll come up with something," replied Cook. "We will not let anybody hurt the lass, by God, we will figure it out. There are enough of us to put our heads together."

Ruby was too traumatised to get out of the cupboard. Cook made her hot tea with sugar to calm her down, then she served her some chicken broth through the small hatchway. She had never seen the girl so terrified. The full horror of her fate had come crashing down upon her. Hearing it happen second hand to Ida had been bad enough. Knowing it would happen to her own person was truly sickening.

Cook tried to catch her eye as she passed the refreshments through. She saw Ruby's usual courageous face now looked defeated, the fire in her eyes extinguished. She was all too aware of what the men were going to do to her, and she was trapped. Seeing her in such a state galvanised Cook to come up with an answer, hook or by crook.

33

SNEED'S TAWDY PUBLICATION

In his office, Kitt was making plans on how to capitalise on Ruby's innocence. He could smell the money already.

"When is the next Gentlemen's Guide to Nightlife due to be published? We need to get a few placements for our fine fillies," he told Jerome his accountant.

"In the next fortnight, Sir," an amoral Jerome replied. He didn't like women and secretly believed that they enjoyed and deserved their lot.

"Find the editor and get him here with a photographer—Pronto. We need to run a prominent feature about our latest offer."

"Yes, Sir."

The editor was a scruffy little runt of a man. He told Jerome that they could only meet in three days because they were so busy. Prostitution was rife, and Robert Sneed's business made him a very wealthy man. His 'guide' was no more than a fortnightly advertisement on where to source the prostitutes who could service particularly explicit needs. It was posted out near and far, from the most sordid to the most sophisticated of institutions in the land. Every fantasy was catered for.

Kitt wanted to take advantage of Ruby's innocence. Old wealthy men were particularly titillated about the deflowering of a virgin girl and would pay enormous sums for the privilege. Kitt could see them lining down the streets, money in hand, to use and abuse the new girl in the fold. All he needed to do was wait for the bruises to die down and claim that the next customer really was the first. Ruby's predictable terror and indignation would add to the illusion wonderfully.

In Angel Meadow, from the age of fourteen girls were deemed fit for work, by seventeen they were used and by twenty they were utterly spent and could hardly make a living on the streets. Now Ruby understood Ida only got business she did because she was prepared to offer a wide range of depraved services—nothing could be too much 'bother if she was to keep a roof over her head.

The younger, the better was Sneed's motto. He loved to advertise the younger ones, boys and girls. The market for them was massive—and lucrative. While Queen Victoria slept under the auspices of ruling a Christian country with sound morals, the subjects of her realm were experiencing the same perversities as the inhabit-ants of Sodom and Gomorrah had; but on the streets of Great Britain.

Tilly had warned Ruby to expect being frogmarched upstairs and forced to take a series of photos in provocative poses. She felt sick at the thought. The forthcoming encounter with Sir Rufus had her petrified, and with him, she had a good idea what she was dealing with. Kitt's clients from the magazine would be an unknown quantity. *How on earth will I cope?* When the time came to see Sneed's grubby photographer, the experience was as demeaning as Tilly said it would be. Ruby did her best to mentally retreat into one of Bianca's happier faraway lands, but was thwarted. The degradation prevailed in her mind.

Ruby felt the clock was ticking. Saturday night loomed large, and there didn't seem to be a plan for the next two days. It would be early on Friday morning when there would be a workable solution to her predicament.

It was Gerhard that dreamed up the wheeze, and it was a good one. Even though the man didn't speak a lot, he listened to everything that was discussed. Well before breakfast, when Kitt would be sleeping off a hangover, the staff gathered in the kitchen. At first, everyone shuffled and looked at their feet with no ideas forthcoming. Then, the solution struck those in the room like a thunderbolt.

"Measles!" Gerhard said, in his thick German accent.

Everybody turned to look at him, needing more elaboration to share his vision.

"If ve tell them she has measles they von't come near her for at least a month. They vill be too scared of getting it too. Ja? Ve fake the spots somehow, and she vill be safe?"

The staff looked at each other, uneasily. Cyril spoke up first with an opinion on the suggestion.

"That's a bloody good plan!"

Reassured, the others nodded in agreement. It was a brilliant plan. Cook set to work immediately on the specifics.

"Find me beets. Them's nice and red. They'll make wonderful spots!"

"It's not beet season, Cook!" they chimed together.

"I know that, but find some, or any red paint and turpentine."

From Cook's mouth to God's ears, Jimmy Townsend, bringing another phantom delivery, was standing at the door, wanting to know what they were discussing.

"What's going on here then? Beets, red paint and turpentine seem mighty strange ingredients for fresh cakes, Cook," he announced in a loud voice.

"Be quiet son, or the 'ole world will 'ear you. Come 'ere."

Jimmy beamed as he was put in the picture. Even his cunning little rapscallion mind would never have thought of it.

"Who are the gorillas at the gate?" he asked Cyril.

"Kitt 'ired 'em in case we try to smuggle Ruby away from 'ere. Them boys is miscreants. Almost broke Jemima's arm for a bit of fun, to make an example of 'er when she walked a bit too near the gate, didn't they? Said it was just a 'friendly warning'. Yeah, right! The women are terrified of 'em now. They want to put the frighteners on 'em alright. Make sure no one 'elps the young 'un."

Jimmy was back within an hour with a genuine delivery. This time it was a bottle of pickled beetroot and a tiny cup of red paint. The compulsive liar in him said with a cheeky smile:

"My uncle's a signwriter, innie!"

"And yer Aunt pickles beets?" said Cook wryly, turning the jar in her hand, eyeing the label trying to identify its exact origin.

"Me cousin works at a hotel!" beamed Jimmy.

With all the ingredients to hand, Cook mixed everything together into a thick reddish-purple concoction. She decanted it into a small suet pudding bowl.

In the hidey-hole, Ruby took off her clothes, and Jemima helped her dab on the concoction. Cook stuck her head through the hatch to check on their progress. She was impressed.

She reached her hand through and gave the girl an onion sliced in half, held together with some butchers' string. There was another suet pudding bowl filled with some yellowy-brown gunge. Ruby had no idea what that was. It mattered not because Cook was about to explain.

"Now this may be disgusting, lass, but it will save yer life. If Kitt or that pig Rufus come in 'ere, you must do what I tell you now. Pay attention! I want you to sniff this onion until your eyes weep a river. In this bowl, it's bone marrow, doesn't it 'alf look like fresh snot. Now, you dab the marrow around yer nose and cough and splutter like a broken-down traction engine. Do yer 'ear me, Ruby?

Ruby nodded her head.

She was now speckled in deep pink from her face to her feet. Her hair was dirty and unkempt. Cook had rubbed some castor oil into her skin to make her look sweaty with the fever. If the men got too close, she would be smelling like soup, but Cook didn't think they would go anywhere near her. She boiled up some pungent cabbage and vinegar in case it helped disguise Ruby's curious aroma.

An impatient voice bellowed down the stairwell again:

"Tilly. Bring the girl!"

Everyone gave Tilly a reassuring smile as she tentatively headed upstairs to explain to Kitt that Ruby was currently 'indisposed'. The next thing they heard were protestations from Mr O'Conner.

"What do you mean 'the measles'?" he roared.

"She is covered top-to-toe in spots, Sir," said Tilly, feigning a look of terror. "I didn't get it as a kid, but my ma said it killed my brother before I was born.

"Do you mean to tell me that I have to cancel Saturday night's introduction because she is sick?" screamed Sir Rufus.

"Tis not my fault, Sir," said Tilly. "The kitchen staff are terrified to catch it. They say she must go. We have so much to do for the other gentlemen booked in this weekend."

"That will not happen," screamed Sir Rufus hysterically, "I have invested way too much. I'll look like the fool in front of the others from my supper club. I want to see her with my own two eyes. I think I am being spun a convenient tale."

"But it's too dangerous, Sir. Like I say, it killed my brother."

"Well, I shall use a posy or hold my breath to shield me from the miasma. I want to see for myself, damn you, woman."

"Does she still sleep under the stairs?" asked Kitt.

"Yes, Sir. You can look in there, you will see her."

"Don't be stupid, Tilly, make her stand outside the door, but don't bring her near us."

"If she lives, how long till she is better?" asked Sir Rufus.

"They say a month, Sir, or until the marks are gone. Six weeks perhaps?" exaggerated Tilly.

It was difficult to tell who was huffing and puffing more at the news, Kitt or Rufus.

Tilly led them to the kitchen. The men stood at the door at what they hoped was a safe distance while Cook called Ruby from her hiding place. Ruby came out looking truly terrible. Her eyes were red and ran with tears. She had more spots then a dalmatian, mucus puthered from her nose. She coughed and choked and coughed again.

Keen to make sure they left as soon as possible, Ruby started to shuffle towards Sir Rufus.

"Get away from me, get away from me. Get back in that hole and don't come out until you are cured."

The two men left the kitchen at a rapid pace as Kitt's voice trailed down the stairs.

"Four weeks on Saturday, Rufus, that's all. You've waited a year. I'll find a string of girls to keep you occupied in the meantime."

The staff were euphoric. It worked. Ruby would be safe for a month. What followed, was the most pleasant time in the kitchen that the staff had ever experienced. Their boss stayed out of their way and left them at peace. Ruby spent a good amount of time reading, but she was also stressed because time was marching on and she still had to escape somehow, without bringing the wrath of Kitt O'Conner down on those she left behind.

She knew that if she could get past the guards, she could escape into the street. She knew that the first place Kitt's goons would look for her was the coffin house because it was the only place that she could shelter. Sleeping on the streets wasn't an option, in the slums, a whole host of horrors could await there. Nobody took strangers in. The workhouse had many of the same abuses as the brothel, with less food.

"Leave it to me, Ruby," Jimmy had said, "I'll get you to safety."

Jimmy didn't know how he would do it, but he knew that time was passing quickly. At least he could give Ruby a glimmer of hope. It would have to do for now. *Maybe I can speak to Constable McGregor if I can find where his new beat is?*

35

THE CROSSING TO LIVERPOOL

The Mediterranean was as smooth as glass on the evening that they sailed from Barcelona. The order to the bridge was full steam ahead.

Diego hoped that the stillness of the water was a good omen for his search for Ruby. Eduardo and Diego were sitting in the Captain's cabin, and Juan was in charge of the ship for now. Juan was no longer a boy, but Diego still remembered the serious child, typical of the oldest son on whose shoulders the entire destiny of the family and business would rest in the future. Diego had been surprised to see Maria at the quayside. She was there to say goodbye and wish them luck.

"Diego, I pray that you will find Ruby. I know in my heart that she is alive."

He sighed. He couldn't look into her eyes without her seeing the tears that he was choking back.

Maria saw Agnes watching them from the upper deck.

"Are you heartbroken?" asked Maria tenderly.

"No, I never loved her," Diego replied. "My flesh was lonely, and I made a bad decision."

"Yes, I have made bad choices as well. You do remember my Englishman, William Eaton?"

He nodded slowly; a slight smile touched his lips.

"Don't be hard on yourself, Diego."

He was rigid, filled with fear and dread. He had not slept, and he couldn't find anything positive on which to focus. Angel Meadow was the filthiest disease-ravaged pit he had ever seen, and the chances of a small child surviving alone were slim. If she had escaped the workhouse or orphanage, she would have been snapped up by an industrialist to work in one of his mills as soon as she was old enough. He had no guarantee that he would find her, and he didn't know where to begin searching. All he knew was that he was to blame. All the guilt came flooding back.

"I must go," whispered Diego, knowing he would feel better when he was under way.

Maria stepped forward and hugged him. Then she arched her back to look at him with earnest. She was convinced of half of what she said next.

"You'll find Ruby, you'll see. I'll be here when you get back."

To reinforce her message, she clutched him towards her with all her might. It felt so warm and comforting, and he didn't want to let go. He held her a moment too long, then kissed her on both cheeks before whispering goodbye.

As they set sail, Diego was in his cabin, sitting in a deep leather chair. He put his head back. He didn't want to talk or think. He just wanted to be.

Exhausted, he dozed in the chair and dreams about Grace floated into his head. He saw her beautiful young face, the radiant smile and the joy in her eyes. She was in a place flooded with light and was wearing the nightdress from their honeymoon. Her ash-blond hair shone like a halo about her head. In his dreamy doze, he thought he heard a banging sound. It became louder and louder, then he woke up fully. It was Eduardo.

"Can I come in? —Diego! —Diego!"

The furious banging continued as he sat up, and as he went over to the door.

"Alright. Alright. Give me a moment." he grumbled, followed abruptly by, "What?"

He was annoyed that his friend had interrupted his dream of his beloved lost wife. If he was honest, he wanted to stay in it and never ever wake up again. The time he spent with Grace was when he was at his most content.

"It is good to be at sea again," said Eduardo.

Diego poured them each a cognac.

"It's almost ten years since we fetched Bianca," he added

Diego nodded, remembering the sewage-riddled streets and the filthy room she lived in.

"My worst fear is that we can't find Ruby," confessed Diego. "Did you ever see that graveyard around St. Michael's? Do you know how many people are buried there? Thousands of corpses wedged on that small hill. Angel Meadow is a place of death. It is a portal to hell, and my child is there somewhere, dead or alive. She is there."

Eduardo let Diego's thoughts tumble out of him. Unburdening his troubled mind had to be a good thing. He dreaded to think about the stress he must have been under. *What if my dear friend is too late to rescue her?*

"Can you imagine if one of your children was living in a place like that and you didn't know it? How hard did we search for Maria to get her out of there? And she was an adult, with a marriage record providing an all-important recent address. It's been over a decade—"

Eduardo nodded his head.

"What am I going to do if I can't find her? How am I going to live knowing that I left her behind? I have betrayed Grace. She looked up to me as a man—a protector. I should never have left her there alone. Surely I could have found a way. I had another precious link to Grace, a true gift from God, and I let her slip through my fingers. How foolish am I? Tell me!"

"Diego, hindsight is a wonderful friend who turns up just too late. Don't be too hard on yourself. I keep telling you that you thought you would be away for a few weeks when you left, not years."

Eduardo's heartening words did not hit their target. All the remorse and regret came flooding back into Diego's soul torturing him. The poor man broke down and wept as his friend looked on, helpless.

"We are going to get through this, my friend. I am going to help you, and we are going to find her together. Everyone on this steamer is willing with all their hearts for you to succeed."

Diego nodded. In such anguish, he couldn't trust his voice. Eduardo had never seen this confident and commanding man so vulnerable, and his heart broke for him. He also knew the Diego of old. *He's a fighter for whom even the most seemingly unsurmountable of problems becomes a mere temporary setback. If anybody has the tenacity to find Ruby, a tiny shiny needle in a filthy haystack, it is my one true friend, Diego. As we sail, he will rest and recover. He is not alone in his quest. We will arrive raring to go, with fire in our hearts. We will all pull together. He will be successful.*

"Now, get some proper rest," Eduardo instructed Diego. "Take the trip to gather your strength, you are going to be fine, and so is Ruby."

With that, Eduardo bade him farewell with a nod and a smile and returned to his cabin.

Diego undressed and climbed into his bunk, and snuggled down under the soft covers. The gentle rocking movement of the steamer was comforting. He drifted off slowly, desperately wanting to dream about Grace again, but his sleep-deprived body switched off, and he fell into a deep sleep, devoid of dreams, pleasant or otherwise.

35

THE LONE FIGURE ON
THE DECK

Diego spent two days resting, and Eduardo gave instructions that nobody disturb him. He ate in his cabin or sat on the deck, gazing at the ocean. Sometimes Eduardo would join him. The men didn't speak much, they were comfortable in each other's silent company. As always, it was enough to offer solace.

On the third day of the sailing, Eduardo could see that Diego's mood was improving. He was always well turned out, and it was heart-warming to see him washed, shaved and dressed in clean clothes once more. He began to patrol the ship with Eduardo, and they spent time speaking to the engineers. Agnes, Diego felt, was best ignored.

He spent hours on the bridge with Juan teaching him about the stars and the old navigation techniques. He monitored the ship's logbook and scrutinised the manifests. The good weather held, and under any other circumstances, it would have been a perfect journey.

Things changed when they sailed into the Irish Sea on the final leg of the route, the approach to Liverpool. The weather deteriorated. The sun and stillness were replaced by light squalls and swell. In the grey gloom, the temperature dropped markedly.

Diego retired to his cabin. His soul had gained some peace in the last few days. He was still filled with fear he might be too late, but there was a sliver of hope, and that, he was clinging on to.

It would be quite some time until Diego finally caught a glimpse of Agnes, towards the end of the crossing. By the morning they would be docking in port. In the dark of night, she walked alone along the deck. Lashed by the wind and spray, she pulled her coat tightly around her as a defence. Her translucent nightdress beneath offered no protection against the elements.

As soon as his gaze met her, she filled him with self-disgust. *How could I let myself be seduced by her? How could it ever be acceptable to sleep with my dead wife's sister— especially when I didn't love her and saw no future in it?* Agnes had managed to drive him to hit her, something that he believed he was never capable of doing to a woman. She was a constant disappointing reminder of his weakness and vulnerability. *Come now, Diego, you have better things to do with your time than be near that harridan.* With his eleven o'clock nightly observation complete and keen to keep his distance, he retired to his cabin. Out of the corner of her eye, a thoughtful Agnes saw him hurry down below deck. *It's now or never, Agnes. It is time to strike!* Despite her pep talk, she was still hesitant. *This is my last chance at a comfortable life with him. I cannot afford to fail.*

Ten minutes later, Agnes subtly rapped her knuckles on Diego's cabin door and then entered without hearing his invitation.

Sitting in his chair dozed off, there he was. A folded map of Manchester had fallen from his hand, and his spectacles had slid halfway down his nose. After carefully sliding the door latch into position, her coat slipped off her shoulders, and she silently placed it on the hook. She smoothed down her gossamer-thin nightdress, specifically chosen because it left nothing to the imagination. Her beauty was the only silver bullet to retain some control over him, and she was determined to use it. She tiptoed across to him, then leaned over and whispered in his ear so softly the two words uttered were barely audible.

"Hello, Diego."

Still drowsy, he opened his eyes slightly and saw a figure of a woman in front of him. Her ash-blonde hair hung straight down her back to her waist. Her nightdress was unbuttoned to her breasts, and with the light behind her, he could see that she was naked underneath it. She had a surreal quality, and he couldn't decide if the vision was real or an apparition. *Grace? Have you come back?*

She walked towards him and sat on his lap and leaned her body closer to his until she was against his chest, heart against heart. The soft tresses of her hair caressed his face.

"Do you remember?" she whispered in his ear, her icy, snow-white cheek almost touching his warm one.

"We were so happy, so good for each other."

"Yes," he murmured, letting his eyes close as he reflected on the delicious memory of his honeymoon.

Agnes felt his right hand move to trace along the gentle curve of her lower back. She reached for his left and caressed it with a lingering kiss. Although he had the toughened hands of a sailor, he could still feel a rough scratch of her split lip against his flesh. The sensation of her lip jolted him out of his sleepy reverie. In a split-second, Agnes's spell was broken.

He shot out of the chair, pushing her away from him forcefully. She stared at him as if he had inflicted a terrible act of brutality upon her.

"You are cruel! For years you wanted me, took me. And now, I am cast aside!" she hissed.

For the first time in years, Diego saw Agnes for who she really was—a selfish, distant gold-digger. She moved towards him. There was no emotion in her eyes. Her angular jaw was clenched, and her mouth formed a thin blue slash across the bottom of her face. Her skin was as white as death itself. Her beauty that had hypnotised him, that similarity to Grace, was now transformed into something menacing. He wanted nothing more to do with her. *I will use her like she used me. We will find Ruby, and then I never want to see that woman again.*

"Get away from me, Agnes. You are here to help locate Ruby in Manchester and nothing more."

"You'll be sorry," she hissed again.

"I am already sorry, Agnes. I am sorry that I invited you to my villa and I am sorry that I allowed you in my bed when I was lonely. I am sorry I betrayed Grace by laying with you. I am sorry I let you abuse my children. You manipulated me for your own benefit. Well, no more!"

"You love me!" she screamed.

"I never loved you, Agnes. You know that."

Her eyes narrowed, and her voice changed back to it's normal, measured, threatening tone.

"You may not love me, Diego, but you will look after me for the rest of my life. I took on your children when you abandoned them for four years. I have helped you raise Bianca for a decade, putting my own happiness on hold. You owe me a significant debt of gratitude."

"No, Agnes, I owe you nothing."

"What will become of me?"

"I am taking you back to Angel Meadow, and I shall leave you where I found you. No doubt you will end up in the lunatic asylum where you belong."

"You can't do that," she screamed at him, "how will I survive alone in the slum?"

"The same way that Ruby has no doubt—and God help your soul if she has not!"

He grabbed her arm and steered her to the door.

"Put your coat on and get out."

She looked at him in defiance.

"Now!" he bellowed.

Sliding back the latch, he swung the door open, then roughly pushed her through. In a furious temper, Agnes pulled her ankle-length coat around her once more and made her way back on deck for some fresh air. After the suffocating atmosphere in Diego's cabin, the breeze would be welcome.

The black and stormy night matched her mood. She hated everybody and everything. She hated her parents whose death resulted in her having to look after her younger sister. She hated Grace. Cheerful, happy-go-lucky Grace. Grace the angel. Grace the favourite. Grace, who found love and marriage at her expense. Secretly, on some unconscious level, she had enjoyed watching Grace suffer and die. *Her thoughtless actions have been the ruin of me. Where was my good fortune? Where was my prince to rescue me from the hell of the Meadow? When Grace died, two women's lives ended, not one.* She had hoped that Diego, the wealthy, healthy Spaniard, would return within weeks. Putting her life on hold was meant to be a 'phase', not her 'future'. *But he took too long to return, didn't he? Gone for years, leaving me to sink, weighed down by the mess of his making. Keeping his children alive killed my society seamstress dream. I might have been able to tolerate carefree and blithe Bianca, but Ruby, the more serious of the two, was a challenging, confrontational child. We failed to build any rapport, only worsening hostility. I am convinced that ungrateful girl thought of me as being pure evil. She owed her life to me, and that was the thanks I got. She deserved the beatings. It would have taught her some manners.*

Over the years as Agnes's life unravelled, she was driven by a demon within her mind that she couldn't control. She gave Ruby the filthiest jobs in the hope that she would get cholera, but she didn't. When Agnes pinched or slapped her, she never yelped in pain. *Why could she not die like so many other unwanted children in the*

Meadow? Oh! That would have been so satisfying, for my tortured, put upon soul.

The steamer was struggling against worsening conditions at sea. The bow of the ship dipped down so low it looked like it could sink into the inky black water at any moment. Then, with the next wave, it miraculously righted itself, its prow rising so high it almost blocked out the low-slung glow of the full moon hiding behind the clouds.

My life would have been very different if I could have got away with putting those children in a sack and thrown them in the River Irk like kittens. Only Bianca's likeness to Grace secured their stay of execution—and the thought of Diego's money one day. Tears of frustration combined with the stinging salty spray from the sea. *Once again, Ruby has spoiled everything for me. Stolen what little joy I had. Diego was to be my husband, and Spain my home. And now, my fate is the Meadow.*

Agnes's cold hands gripped the icy metal of the leeward rail. Huge waves of confusion finally overwhelmed her delicate mental state. *Diego loves me. I know he does. He will be sorry he let me go. He will grieve for me.*

She clambered onto the first rung on the railings, and in that moment, she was sure. She swung her legs over the top, then placed her heels carefully on the black metal hull, her arms outstretched behind her, grabbing the rail as she precariously balanced for a few seconds.

She felt all alone—but she wasn't. Before the storm reached its peak, Juan was checking everything was shipshape up on deck.

"Agnes!" he screamed.

It was too late. She jumped. A terrified Juan looked over the rail. Below, the frosty ice queen looked angelic. Face down, her blonde hair fanned out, and her white night-clothes floated around her. Her arms were still stretched out wide.

Juan sounded the klaxon and screamed orders to put the ship into reverse. It might have been the textbook re-sponse, but in such rough seas, any attempt at rescue would be doomed. Their progress suggested that the ship was already a nautical mile away. There was noth-ing that could be done for Agnes.

The ship docked in Liverpool, and they caught a train to Manchester. Diego, Eduardo and Juan sat in a compart-ment by themselves. The news of Agnes's death weighed heavy on the little gathering. They watched the city dissolve into the countryside. Diego saw the Pendle Hills in the distance, and he remembered the little rented cottage where he and Grace spent their honey-moon.

It was the best month he had ever lived. He remembered them lying in bed in the sunlight, reading to each other in the firelight, hiking through the woods, wading in the crystal clear water. He so loved her wonder and celebra-tion at everything big and small. *How she would have loved Bianca and Ruby, how she would have celebrated the miracle of children.* He would always have kept her safe, he would have protected her from everything evil. But he didn't, and he spent the rest of his days paying the price for that. He hoped that there would be no more deaths on his conscience.

36

THE DESPERATE NEED FOR A PLAN

Jimmy Townsend walked every morning to buy stale loaves from Mr Hammond's bakery, situated in a far cheerier part of Manchester, Cheetham Hill. It was a couple of miles north of Angel Meadow. Then he wheeled his barrow down towards the slum to sell his wares. The Meadow bakers cut their bread flour with chalk and alum, a cunning wheeze to eke out more profit from the unsuspecting. Most slum-dwellers could stomach it, but it tasted awful, and if you were weakened with disease, it had the tendency to poison you—fatally.

In comparison, Jimmy's stale, unadulterated bread was delicious. Although three days old and desperately dry, he told his punters its rigidity made it ideal for dunking in broth. If he didn't shift it quickly, there would be signs of mould within a day, so he was glad he had a roaring trade and always sold out. His little business, albeit humble, afforded him a modest income. After he bought his stock, there was enough money left each week to rent a small room in the backyard of a house owned by a Jewish family in Cheetham. In fact, it was the Weiss's who had given him the idea to launch his tiny baking empire in the first place.

Mrs Weiss taught him to give the housewives a few tips on how to create a tasty meal with it. Dip it in hot sweet tea for a treat. Add onion and cheese over it and toast it in the oven and there was a warming evening meal. Break some into hot milk, bash it with a fork and hey presto, porridge. It gave him plenty of barrow-boy banter, which he yelled out like a foghorn. Jimmy's popular stall was well-liked because his frugal recipes worked, and he had a sincere interest in his customers.

He had opened the stall in the hope that Ruby would one day come and help him. Also, having the occasional unsold loaf with him provided his delivery boy cover story to get past the goons at Kitt O'Connor's gate.

He was at a loss on how to rescue her from Kitt. The measles hoax was a good temporary solution, but the other ideas he had felt desperate and unfeasible.

He could approach the scuttlers to get her out, but most of them frequented the place and would want to take advantage of Ruby anyway. Worse, they would expect a ransom of sorts or protection money to stop her being smuggled back in. As he had none, the idea was doomed. Constable McGregor was out of the Meadows area now, and Sir Rufus had bribed so many coppers down at the local police station, they would laugh Jimmy out of the building. The two guards at the gate were the brutal henchmen of Kitt O'Connor. He might be able to come and go, but Ruby certainly couldn't. His only other hope was Tilly, but he was sure that she was being watched very closely. He had a reason to chat with Cook, but not her.

It was early evening, and three tired Spaniards booked into Diego's home-from-home in Manchester, his expensive suite at the Grand Hotel. He'd advised they would be comfortable there, and it would be an excellent base from which to explore. He reminded them how well it had served him when he found Maria—with success.

Tired and hungry from the fraught journey, they agreed to retire for an hour to freshen themselves, then reconvene for a hearty room service meal and work out the final details of their rescue mission.

"Diego, you know Manchester better than any of us. Where should we begin our search for Ruby?" asked Eduardo.

Keen to finally make a proper start, an upbeat Diego began to share the strategy he had been mulling over during their long sea passage.

"Here is my view, Gentlemen. Tomorrow morning, I shall visit the tea room where Grace and I used to meet. I'll see if I know anybody still working there. They are well connected to the people in the local community. As you are less familiar with the area, could you two please go together to Manchester City Police station? Their bobbies' beats cover a wider area than the Meadow. I've written down the address. Here."

He slid a note between their dinner plates. Eduardo put it in his wallet for safekeeping.

"They may have some information for us or advice on where to look. I expect they will also have the jurisdiction to inspect the workhouse and orphanage admissions. That research will provide some vital clues, and help us rule out some avenues for inquiry."

Juan and Eduardo nodded in agreement.

"Si. Si."

Diego's eyes and voice lowered as he continued.

"I will also speak to the vicar at St Michael and All Angels—and ask to inspect the burial records."

Feeling the implication of his last comment draining the life out of the room, he returned to more practical matters.

"Let us wake early at seven and meet for a hearty breakfast. There will be a long day ahead. We can run our errands and meet back here at five to discuss our findings?"

All in agreement, they finished their meal and retired to the suite's sitting room. Hugging large brandies, they stared in silence at the face of the ornate carriage clock slowly ticking on the mantlepiece.

37

BACK AT THE TEA SHOP

As day broke, the weather was foul, dark and brooding. The howling wind whipped up all the dirt and soot from the industrial areas. The three Spaniards, with their tanned skin and strange fashions, were immediately recognisable as foreigners—and after centuries of warfare, the English didn't like foreigners very much. Diego hoped that this wouldn't frustrate their search. They had plenty of money in their pockets, aware that they may have to incentivise their informants.

Diego's cab dropped him in front of the tea room in Angel Street. It cheered his aching heart to see it was still open. Very little had changed since his first visit all those years ago, but the owner, John Coggan, was no longer there. In his place behind the counter was a young lady, who he guessed was around eighteen years of age. She was brash and loud, and she seemed to know everybody by name. The place had never been spotless, but it seemed to have suffered from considerable neglect over the years. The same tables stood against the walls, but they were rickety and old, and most of the crockery placed upon them was chipped and tarnished with deep brown tea stains around the rim. He was so engrossed in the place he hadn't noticed he was blocking the aisle, and a queue of people was beginning to form. Seeing she was missing out on trade, the girl yelled out:

"Sir! What are you after? Sir! I haven't got all day! Tea is it?"

As the stranger stepped closer, with a second look, she could now place him. *Yes, I know him, alright. He was that flash foreign sort who tipped well.*

"Oi! Aren't you the man from Spain that visited a few years ago? Sailor, weren'tchya, I reckon? Can't miss ya, not with a tanned face like that— foreign-looking. I knew straight away."

There was something so familiar about this girl, but he couldn't quite place her.

"I am sorry, Miss," he apologised. "I fear although you may know me, I cannot bring you to mind."

"O' course you remember me, love!" she said at the top of her lungs. "I am Kathleen Coggan. John's daughter. I showed you where Grace lived when you came back to fetch her. Must have been about ten years ago? You gotta remember summat as important as finding the sister of yer dearly departed wife looking after yer daughters, Sir?"

Daughters. She said, daughters. Her cavernous memory seemed as good as one of those new-fangled photographic images when it came to recording details from the past. He allowed himself a faint glimmer of hope that Ruby was alive. The pieces began to fall into place for Diego. This was the jabbering child that had taken him to Grace's house all those years ago. She hadn't changed at all, still loud and obnoxious, and always knowing everybody's business. *Perfect. If anyone knows what happened to Ruby, surely, she will.*

"Oh, yes, Kathleen. Now, I remember you. I cannot thank you enough for your help that day!" Diego turned the dial of his charm setting to full power.

"I'll have one of your finest cups of tea."

Kathleen raised an eyebrow, and he considered toning down the flattery a notch.

He handed over half a crown for the beverage and Kathleen was delighted when he told her to keep the change. *I shall help this Spanish fella again I think. It's definitely worth my while!*

Knowing the tip would buy him the few seconds of her attention, as he picked up the tea, he said softly:

"It's a delicate matter, but I would like to speak to you when you have a free moment. I need your help again, Miss Coggan."

"Well, ya know me, I know everything that 'appens in the Meadow, dun I. Tell ya what. Come back at the lull after elevenses and before the noon rush. I'll take my break then."

Eduardo and Juan walked into the city police station on Newton St. The place was crowded with bobbies and people who represented a cross-section of the population. There were the well-dressed gangster types, sneering, trying to be intimidating. Formerly loving couples, hauled in from the streets for drunken fighting, continued their domestic disputes in full view of the charge room. Ragged children dragged in for basic mischief were eyeing up more pockets ripe for picking.

There was so much noise that Eduardo and Juan couldn't hear each other speaking. The situation seemed hopeless. It looked like it would take them hours to get to the front of the queue and talk to somebody. However, they had no alternative, and so they stayed. An hour and a half later, they got to the head of the processing queue, and a polite policeman asked if he could be of any help.

"Yes, Sir," replied Eduardo. "Officer, there used to be a little girl who lived in this area called Ruby Alaniz, and we are looking for her."

"What is your business with the child, Sir?" asked the constable.

"Her father, a Spanish sailor, Diego Alaniz, wishes to locate her. They lost touch when he was away at sea."

"It's an unusual surname, that's for sure, but it means nothing I'm afraid. A lot of folks live here, I can only place the wrong 'uns by name, of course. When did she live here?"

A concerned Eduardo continued with his best optimistic voice, despite feeling nothing of the sort.

"About ten years ago. She would be fourteen now."

"Sir, I am sorry that was a long time ago. I don't know if we can help you, but I'll try. Please wait."

After what felt like an eternity, the policeman returned to advise the two anxious visitors what he had found.

"I have asked every constable that is on duty, and they can't remember that far back. Your best bet is to find someone who walked their beats around the Meadow back then. Most of the poor buggers are dead thanks to the scuttling. Those gangland lads are cold-blooded murderers the lot of 'em."

Eduardo and Juan gave each other a nervous glance.

"I have got something you can follow up on. An officer who spent many a year patrolling the Meadow is one of thirty-nine men stationed at Salford Borough Police Station. Ask for Constable McGregor. He might well be your only clue. Here's his officer number and the address."

Eduardo slotted the second precious piece of paper into his wallet.

Diego returned to the tea room at eleven-fifteen. The wait to talk to Kathleen had been arduously long.

"Take over for a bit, Janey, will ya? There aren't too many punters. I've got a bit of personal business to deal with."

An exhausted-looking Jane stared at her, sighing as she saw all the empty cups littering every table. *There might not be a lot of people, but there was still a lot of work, Kathleen!*

"You said daughters when we spoke earlier. So, it's true there were twins?"

"Aye. Grace had two girls. To tell ya the truth, Mister Diego, the last time I 'eard anything was when Miss Agnes left with you. Never took much notice after that. Not my business is it?"

Diego was surprised at her last comment. It seemed Kathleen had an eternal interest in everyone's business!

"It's a bit 'azy now, but I did 'ear that Ruby was in 'ospital, then she disappeared. I dunno if the undertaker took 'er or the parish guardians, but she did a flit, and I didn't 'ear no more about her."

"Thank you very much, Kathleen. At least I definitely know I have—or had— a second daughter. That is very helpful."

Diego thanked her kindly and stood up to leave.

"Very helpful, you say?"

Opportunistic as ever, Kathleen held out her hand. He put a pound note into it. She kept her hand open and wiggled her fingers:

"Inflation, Mister."

Diego counted out another pound. She kept looking at him expectantly, then she sighed and put the money into her pocket.

Nothing about Kathleen had changed in ten years.

Diego's optimism was raised another notch when his visit to browse the burial records for St Michael and the Angels parish drew a blank. He hoped it was another tick in the box towards finding his daughter alive. *I wonder what Eduardo and Juan have found out?*

With eagerness, he strode to his cab, smiling all the way back to the Grand.

38

FINDING THE BOBBY ON THE BEAT

The three men met again at the hotel at five o'clock as agreed. They exchanged information over a few glasses of fine Highland single-malt whisky. It made a welcome change from the Spanish brandy.

The next day they agreed they would find Constable McGregor. They all felt he knew something important, even though they had never met him.

The cab ride to Salford Constabulary headquarters took an age. Manchester's streets were buzzing with trams, omnibuses, coaches, wagons, carts and people, although it was difficult to see them clearly with all the raindrops trickling down the windows. Eduardo and Juan were thankful to see the station was not as chaotic as the Manchester City Police HQ had been the day before.

Eduardo began explaining the situation, and another efficient officer offered to help them.

"We have received information that Constable McGregor, PC 35A, worked in the Meadow area and he may have some information that could help us."

"I am sorry, Sir," replied the crestfallen officer. "Constable McGregor—he no longer works here."

The three Spaniards hoped he had not added to the fatality statistics for the crusade against the scuttlers.

"He retired some months ago. But yes, if anybody would have the information, it would be him. He lives about twenty minutes' walk away. Given we're looking for a missing daughter, I'll send one of the lads with you right now to show you the way to his house."

The officer slid a wooden panel to one side and popped his head through the hatch, then yelled

"Jonesy, Come here, lad! A little job for you."

Diego was overwhelmed by the officer's kindness. When he turned back to face him, the Spaniard wanted to show his gratitude.

"Can I pay you, Sir?" he asked.

"No, Mr Alaniz. Serving the community is our job. You put your money away before you get me into trouble for accepting a bribe!"

"Ah, Jonesy. Take these gentlemen to see Mac McGregor, they need his help with an open case over at the Meadow. A missing daughter belonging to Mr Alaniz. Take them there, will you?"

"Yes, Sir. Of course."

Jonesy looked at the worsening storm clouds through the barred windows, disappointed to be dragged from some nice, dry paperwork duties he had carefully organised for himself that day.

"Do you chaps mind if I get my overcoat first. It looks nasty out there."

The three men had no complaints at all.

Constable McGregor's little home was a narrow two-up, two-down mid-terraced house with a tiny square of paving for a garden. All the beautiful bobbing blooms outside were contained in a colourful window box. The windows were clean, and the door was painted a bright yellow creating a cheerful impression, despite the overcast weather. All the homes on the street were well maintained.

Constable Jones took the black door knocker in his hand and gave three authoritative taps. The other three men stood a couple of paces behind him on the pavement, speechless, their hearts in their mouths.

They could see something moving behind the stained-glass. A woman with grey hair and rosy cheeks answered the door, a little bewildered to see four visitors turn up unannounced.

"Good afternoon, Polly. You're looking in fine fettle! Is Mac there? These three fellows need his 'elp. It's about a missing girl from the Meadow. Sergeant Cottrell down at the station, thinks Mac might know something."

Diego stepped forward and supplied more details as he respectfully removed his hat.

"Good day, Señora. It is me who needs your husband's help. I am truly grateful for any assistance. It's my daughter who is lost."

"Och, well we can't have that, can we? You fellows had better come in."

She led them into the little parlour at the front and offered them a seat before stepping back into the hallway. Eduardo, Juan and Diego squashed themselves onto a small couch. Jones decided to stand, keen to make a sharp exit and get back to his paperwork.

"Mac, Jonesy is 'ere, with some men who say they need your 'elp,"

The parlour was small, filled with books and bric-a-brac on shelves. Cramped with them all crowding in there, it was still inviting and warm. Diego heard the gentle thud of some footsteps as they made their way downstairs.

Jonesy introduced the strangers then promptly left them to explain further.

"Tea for you gentlemen?" asked Polly

"Si, Señora," they replied in unison.

"So, what brings you to our neck of the woods?" laughed the big Scotsman. "I don't often get people coming all the way from Spain to visit me."

Laughter broke out as Polly served tea and biscuits, pretending not to listen to the conversation, but secretly monitoring every word.

After the polite chit-chat, Diego was desperate to turn the conversation to Ruby's whereabouts.

"Señor, I don't know if you can remember a young woman called Grace Edwards, si?"

"Yes, of course, I remember young Gracie. I knew her from a wee girl, and her sister Agnes. Good family the Edwards'. Their ma and pa were great people, but the family fell on hard times. The father was viciously attacked for his pay packet. The mum was a fighter—stabbed her husband's murderer that night. Yes, buried them next to each other under the flags somewhere. But that was a long time ago."

"Señor, I mean Mac, were you still policing Angel Meadow when Grace died? It would be around 1872?"

"Yes, I was. She was so bright. She could cheer up the whole street just by walking down it. But the sister, Aggie, she was otherwise. Yes, Gracie married, on the spur of the moment, all hush-hush. A rich man, foreign, which I suppose is you, Diego?"

He nodded.

"That Aggie, she was frightfully jealous of her sister, now wasn't she, Mac?" said Polly.

"Oh, crikey aye!" said the old man. "I never understood why. Och, Aggie was beautiful, and she coulda had any man, but she was hard and miserable all the time. Put them off in droves it did. Nae laddie would take her on."

Mac leaned forward, his eyes narrowing as he looked directly at Diego.

"The thing is I canna understand why you abandoned Gracie just as suddenly as you were wed? Kathleen told me she seemed smitten with her new husband."

Polly added:

> "Aye, Kath told me Gracie said it was mutual. Besotted, she said. But that husband of hers just vanished without a bye or leave as soon as he found Gracie was expectin'."

They were talking about Diego as if he wasn't there. Clearly, they had formed a strong opinion about him, and it wasn't a good one. He knew that if he didn't explain his absence, Mac and Polly would divulge nothing. Clearly, being an absent husband and father was not the best way to inspire trust in the law-abiding McGregor's.

> "Señor, Yes, I am the man who married Grace. I lived for her. She was my everything. But we were to be most unlucky in love."

He cleared his throat.

> "Looking back, it was more like an elopement than a marriage. We didn't want to wait for a church service and besides, Agnes was working away. We went to the Register Office in the morning, and by the evening we were beginning our month-long honeymoon in the Lake District. Afterwards, we returned to Manchester to tell Agnes our news. This was around the time of a great uprising in my homeland. It was just before the start of the Carlist war—a civil war."

An experienced policeman, Mac was able to listen and show no emotion on his face whatsoever. He'd been told many a sad story by cads and bounders in his time, and he took nothing at face value. His detached expression threw Diego a little, but he forced himself to carry on. He caught Eduardo's eye, and he gave him a reassuring smile.

"While I was away, John Coggan at the tea shop, agreed to act as my post restante address. On my return to the Meadow, Kathleen brought me a week-old telegraph that summonsed me to Spain so that the government could use my ships in the fight against the rebel uprising. It would take me a week to get back home. I was going to be in trouble with the authorities for not complying with their orders."

Eduardo added:

"Diego and I, along with many others, were against the war and we resisted the requisition order for as long as possible. The Duke of Madrid impounded our ships and put us in gaol. It was almost five years before the courts freed us and we got our ships back."

Diego continued with the explanation.

"I sent some letters, but after a while, prisoners were denied that privilege. The government was concerned about information being leaked to the rebels. I am sure many people decided I had

perished at that point. Eduardo and I came back
to fetch Grace as soon as we could."

His voice began to crack with emotion. Mac was starting
to believe he was not an errant husband after all, and
genuinely cared for the poor dead girl.

"When I arrived, I found—"

He choked up and fell silent. Images of Grace flitted
through his consciousness. Eduardo had to continue.

"—Agnes blurted out to him that Grace was dead."

Finally, Mac and Polly showed they had empathy with
the widower.

"I never saw her again. I can't even visit the grave.
It was lost when a landslide struck St Michael's
Flags."

He told them the story of Agnes and Bianca and her evil
deception. They thought it best not to mention Agnes's
disappearance overboard.

"I have to find Ruby, Señor. I'll never rest until I
do find her—"

He swallowed hard; his eyes watered:

"—dead or alive."

Mac knew precisely what to do and took control of the situation.

"Be a treasure and get me a pen and paper, Polly, will you?"

Silence fell in the room as she passed one of his old notebooks to him along with a fountain pen he'd been given as a retirement gift. The nib scratched along the paper as Mac jotted down some details. Diego thought he looked more like a doctor writing a prescription than a policeman. *Please let him have the answer to what breaks my heart.*

"It is too late today," advised Mac, "but tomorrow, go to the Angel Street market place, about ten o'clock, no earlier. Look for a young lad called Jimmy Townsend. He made friends with Ruby the day she was admitted to hospital. Him and his Ma, Ida looked after her when Agnes vanished with Bianca."

At the mention of the hospital, Eduardo and Diego looked at each other. It was another shred of confirmation tying together the many threads of the stories surrounding Ruby's whereabouts.

"Now, Jimmy sells bread from a barrow. You can hardly miss him. Sings out like a canary with his sales patter. He has the brightest red hair and freckles. He's a bit of a rough diamond, but he has a heart of gold when it comes to looking after

Ruby. He will know what's happened to her. When I left Gould Street Station down on the Meadow, I lost touch with her."

He passed them his notes and gave them a moment to read it.

"You got that?"

"Si. Gracias, Mac!" said a relieved Diego.

Once more, Diego allowed himself to believe that Ruby was still alive.

"If I think of anything else, I'll leave a message at the Grand."

The grateful trio returned to the suite feeling triumphant. Tomorrow could not arrive too quickly.

39

THE RUSE IS RUMBLED

Almost a fortnight had passed, and Kitt O'Connor was frustrated. *No one else seems to have caught this highly infectious disease from the girl. And Doctor Jervis said a youngster might be clear of it in a lot less than a month. I think I might have been spun a fine tale. I need that advert releasing and the bookings coming in. If a photographer can fake the appearance of a ghostly spectre in an image, they can fake the disappearance of spots with a dusting of talcum powder. As soon as Sir Rufus and her pals are done with her, she needs to start earning her keep. I am not running a charity for waifs and strays here. If Rufus nags me about the matter one more time, I swear I will explode.*

An agitated Kitt charged into the kitchen with Tilly close at his heels.

"Get the girl in here!" he ranted.

"But what if you catch the disease, Mr O'Conner?"

"Never mind that. I want her here with her clothes off ready for the photos."

"But, Sir," interrupted Cook, the girl is still—"

She didn't finish her sentence. His face was barely inches away from hers, and his was bright red with fury,

"Don't lie to me, Cook! If she doesn't undress herself here and now, I will get Gerhard to drag her out and strip her!"

"Calm down, Sir." cooed Tilly.

"You know how professional I am. I have worked for you for many years. Let me inspect the girl. You can avoid the disease, and you won't strike her in temper. Rufus won't take kindly to receiving damaged goods."

It made sense. If he dared touch Ruby, Sir Rufus would murder him. If he broke the contract and the deal fell through, Kitt couldn't afford to give back the money— he had already frittered it away on drink and cigars.

Kitt wanted to be sure that Ruby would be advertised in every entertainment magazine in the city, ready for her appearance 'on the circuit' in two weeks. Tilly went into the cupboard.

"Ruby, if we lie, he will come in here himself and drag you out. Then we have no idea of what he will do to you. He will humiliate you in front of the whole kitchen, and more. Trust me. I know what I am saying. He has done it to me."

Ruby nodded. Tilly's face emerged from out of the cupboard, smiling,

"Just as you said, Sir. The girl shows no signs of being ill. She's fully recovered."

Kitt said nothing, annoyed about the shenanigans going on, but also relieved there finally seemed to be light at the end of the tunnel. Nothing had been simple since the child arrived. Sir Rufus was a permanent irritation, and the only reason he was continuing with the plan was that she was going to make him a lot more money in the future. The sooner Ruby got out of the kitchen and into the bedroom, the better.

Sir Rufus walked into Kitt's office, displaying his usual arrogance.

"So, is she ready?" he asked sarcastically.

"I have some good news for you, Rufus, indeed she is. You can tell your friends she will be available this Saturday—two weeks earlier than promised." said a smug Kitt before he drew on his fat Cuban cigar.

"I hope I can share in some of the profits after Saturday." said the evil politician.

"Of course, we are old friends. There's a good three years left in her," nodded Kitt.

"Perhaps you can offer me a few nights on the house to thank me for bringing you the golden goose?" Rufus gave a charming smile.

"As soon as your outstanding debts are settled, we can talk about perks, Rufus. I have paid Sneed a fortune to advertise her in every entertainment rag in this city. If you want to make money out of the girl, you'll have to pay towards the marketing costs. The edition going out tomorrow cost me a damn fortune. I am having first dibs on that revenue stream."

Sir Rufus nodded in resignation. Everyone knew about his debt problems, and it was severely curtailing his fun. He decided to turn his mind to brighter matters—planning Saturday night.

I'm pretty sure I won't drug her for myself. I want her fresh and alert when I experience her. But for all the others to have their chance, I might have to later. After three or four, it might be better if she was more—compliant. I'll ask at my private club what the gents prefer.

40

EAVESDROPPING ON WHITEY

Over the past week or so, Jimmy had enjoyed a run of good days on his barrow. Those evenings, he would treat himself to a drink at a more sophisticated establishment than the spit-and-sawdust Weaver's Arms. The Prince of Wales catered for the lower-middle class market. It was an excellent place to sit and watch the world go by, without worrying a light-fingered little oik might snaffle the day's takings. The canny market traders in the area picked up a lot of business tips just by listening. Jimmy was no exception. He had also made a few mates and enjoyed a chinwag with a nicer class of bloke.

That night, there was a bawdy crowd of chaps standing about the bar. *Flicking through a tawdry penny dreadful no doubt.* Jimmy wasn't focusing on their conversation, but he did pick up bits and pieces of it. He had no choice; they were speaking so loudly.

"Aye up, Whitey, where'dya pick up that ol' rag then?" said Smithy.

"Hilda's gonna break yer neck if she sees you looking at them pictures."

"A man's entitled to look, innie? I ain't touching 'er, am I?" joked Whitey. "Aah! Listen to this, fellas—fourteen years old. I remember when Dotty was fourteen, and she could make a fortune if she was smart. She's a bit past it now."

The men roared with laughter, and the barmaid gave them an eagle-eyed death stare for their cheek.

"Nah, chaps. I 'ave a daughter that age. Let it be. Tis disgustin'. I am going 'ome.'" said Smithy

"Aaah! It says she is an exotic beauty too!" shouted Whitey with delight.

"Is there a price on her, I've been paid me overtime! I might be able to have a couple of goes at it!" yelled Bert.

The men howled with laughter.

"Is she a local?" asked Bert.

"Not with a name like this one," said Whitey.

"Well 'urry up, will ya! What's 'er name then?"

"Ruby. Ruby Alaniz."

Jimmy spun around in his chair.

"What did ya say her name was?"

"Why? Ya interested, boy?" enquired Bert.

"Who wouldn't be?" Jimmy said, trying to remain calm.

"Ruby Alaniz!" shouted Whitey, "It says here she will be available from Saturday night down at Kitt O'Connor's.

A furtive Jimmy Townsend breezed out of the pub, perspiration pouring down his face. He was only a young lad on his own, and he was going to free Ruby from that brothel if it killed him. He had no choice. There was no other way. He was riddled with guilt. *Why did I allow it to continue for such a long time? I am a dreadful coward. What if I am too late?*

41

THE EMPTY SPACE AT THE SMITHFIELD MARKET

When he got back from the boozer that night, Jimmy could hardly sleep at all. Eventually, he drifted off. The next thing he heard was Mrs Weiss shouting his usual morning wake-up call at six. He was so exhausted he didn't want to lift his head from the pillow. Much to his later annoyance, he discovered he had dozed off again. He woke up in a flap at gone twelve. Making it to his usual place at the market at three-thirty in the afternoon, he was not sure why he even bothered to go. He was too late to buy up much stale bread from Hammond's bakery, and the smog-filled gloom made looking for any ad hoc afternoon labouring opportunities rather dismal.

He arrived at his Smithfield pitch to find three men loitering where his barrow would normally stand. He nodded nervously, pensively, trying to suss out the situation. The fellows looked like they were waiting for him. He could see that they were foreigners, and he became anxious trying to work out who could be baying for his blood this week. *I've not told anyone about my plan to rescue Ruby. Kitt O'Conner's thugs couldn't have guessed, could they?* His heart knocked loudly against his chest as they began walking towards him. *I've had plenty of roughing-ups in my lifetime, and I don't want another one—especially if it's three against one. God, if you're watching a lowly sinner like me, I swear I have not wronged anybody recently, and I owe no money.* Jimmy was not a god-fearing man, but he was wary of newcomers to the area, especially when they were eyeing up his pitch.

"Good afternoon," said Juan extending a friendly hand towards the lad, confusing him terribly. "We are looking for a chap called Jimmy Townsend."

There was no mistaking Jimmy. There he stood with is bright red hair bursting out from under his cap and a mass of freckles adorning his cheeks.

Cautiously, Jimmy confirmed who he was with a nod.

"We've been waiting since ten o'clock this morning for you to arrive," said Juan. "It's a good job we stayed."

"Aye. I usually start at ten. 'Ad a bit of trouble getting 'ere today. You're not from around these parts, are ya? Who told you I'd be 'ere?"

"Constable McGregor. You might know him as 'Mac'?" said Diego.

Jimmy relaxed. Mac was a good guy who wanted to keep Jimmy on the straight and narrow. *It must be a business opportunity.*

"My name is Diego."

"'Ow can I 'elp you? Are yer looking for bread for yer restaurant or summat?" asked Jimmy.

"No. But I am looking for a lost girl. Mac thinks you might be able to shine a light on her current location." answered Diego, praying that Jimmy would have information.

"Why?"

"I am her father," said Diego. "She was abandoned many years ago, and I have come to find her."

"What's 'er name, this girl o' yours?"

"Ruby. Ruby Alaniz."

Tears of relief formed in Jimmy's eyes and he wiped them away with the back of his hand, ashamed to show his emotion in front of the swarthy strangers. *Maybe*

God is looking out for me after all. I swear I'll never sin again! The lad's sensitive response made Diego panic, but he needn't have.

"Yes! I know where she is, Sir. And I am beyond thrilled that you are here!"

Dusk was settling over the market, and some of the vendors were moving on. Eduardo suggested they find a quieter place to speak. They walked to the Prince of Wales on Jimmy's recommendation and squashed into a private booth in the snug bar, where they could talk.

It took Jimmy an hour to tell them Ruby's story. He told them everything she had been through, the accident, living with his ma, Ida, being kidnapped by Sir Rufus, and now her terrible situation at Kitt O'Connor's brothel.

Diego was incandescent with rage for Agnes beyond what he previously believed he was capable of. *If I had known the details of Ruby's life, I would have throttled the witch years ago, she wouldn't have needed to jump overboard my ship to end her shame!* But he hadn't known, and the old familiar guilt settled over him once more.

"What are you going to do?" asked Jimmy.

"What I should have done a long time ago," answered Diego, "I am going to fetch her. Now."

The four men made their way over to O'Connor's, Jimmy leading the way and Diego embroidering the details onto their rough plan as they walked.

42

THE STRANGERS WITH THE SPECIAL REQUEST

It was Friday night, usually a good time for business at Kitt's brothel. It was still early, but a few men from the Manchester Ship Canal's many warehouses were already settling in for the fun ahead. The lights were set low, and the girls were working the room. Kitt O'Connor sat in his designated seat in the far corner assessing the scene. *Why can't these men recognise my girls' false smiles and fake laughter? I suppose they don't care about the hint of misery as long as they are available? Well, business is business and as long as the punters keep opening their wallets and the girls their legs, well, frankly, I don't care. They're not here for the chit-chat, are they, Kitt, you fool?*

He was doing calculations in his head. If business didn't pick up by eleven o'clock, he would have to push the girls to add a few special 'pricier' services on the menu to keep the lads there longer.

"Tilly!" he growled just loud enough for her to hear.

"Yes, Sir," she answered as she sat on his lap, smiling like a Cheshire cat.

"Tell the girls to work the lads longer. We need the cash tonight. Get them to offer a few extras if they want them."

"Of course, Kitt," answered Tilly

Tilly had been forced to flee from home when she was not much older than Ruby. Her father abused her terribly. She pawned her mother's ring, which paid for a week or two in the doss house, but she knew the money would run out soon, and it did. A couple of the girls told her to call at Kitt's if she wanted to avoid the workhouse. It seemed such a natural choice at the time. She told herself with a few stiff drinks inside her she'd cope and that it wouldn't be forever. By now, she'd led that existence for a few years, despite knowing that she would die young if she continued. Disease or violence would bring about her premature end. She had experienced Kitt's brutality when he punched her in the stomach for angering a good customer. She'd been a favourite of Sir Rufus's since the death of Ida. She knew that the abuse was escalating and would reach a point where she would be too damaged, too scarred to work. Kitt told her once not to worry saying 'The lads don't look at the fireplace as they stoke the fire', meaning that the simple answer was to sell her for more and more demeaning services where a pretty face was less important.

On hearing the bell ring, Gerhard and Tilly opened the front door to two men. By the way they were dressed, she recognised that they were foreigners—rich ones. Diego and Eduardo were not shocked by what they saw. In the early years of their business, they had dragged a lot of their crew members out of places like this. Brothels were the same all over the world, and so were sailors.

Diego spoke first.

> "Is Kitt O'Connor here. We're new in town, and Dotty in the Prince of Wales said he could help us experience some of the fine Manchester nightlife. She showed us Robert Sneed's brochure."

Eduardo continued:

> "Yes. We're looking for a nice little memento of our time in England. You know us sailors have a girl in every port. I am sure Kitt has just the right one for us."

> "Mr O'Connor's there. In the corner," said Tilly and nodded her head towards him. "May I take your 'ats and coats?"

> "No," replied Diego and Eduardo in unison, "we can manage, thank you."

Tonight will go a lot quicker if these two are big spenders.

Diego sauntered over to Kitt, doing his best to appear nonchalant. Kitt had enough time to assess that this was a very wealthy man. *Excellent. He'll top up my coffers if I can get him the girl he's looking for.*

"Please, sit down," said Kitt pointing to the two chairs beside him with his cigar.

"We prefer more privacy," urged Diego, looking over his shoulder. "We don't like people knowing our business. Blackmailing a wealthy gent is such an ugly practice. You can never be too careful." answered Diego.

After that, he left the speaking to Eduardo as planned. They had anticipated he would be more cool-headed. Sniffing they had oodles of money, Kitt was happy to oblige.

"Let us go to my office, gentlemen." nodded Kitt.

He stood up and began walking through the labyrinthine house until he reached the door that led into his study.

"I take it you're here on business?"

"Yes," answered Eduardo.

"What brings you here?" asked Kitt.

"We have one night here in Manchester, and we want to celebrate closing a monumental deal. Really mark the occasion."

"I see. And what sort of girl are you looking for?"

"Well, we perused Sneed's Guide to Manchester Nightlife, and we couldn't decide who was the most delectable."

Kitt smirked:

"We have many girls here. I am sure we can arrange something to meet your every need."

"The thing is. We are looking for a very young girl. Only just legal." said Eduardo.

"Ah, that young. I understand. It's such a sweet experience deflowering the freshest of blooms. A very rare and precious treat. Of course, that will cost quite a bit more." advised Kitt, keen to stress their wished could definitely be accommodated if they were prepared to pay.

Eduardo took a thick bundle of five-pound notes from his briefcase and flicked at the corners like a polished card dealer at a casino. A tantalised Kitt began to tot up how many there were. *Well, well, well. Tonight is going to be very lucrative after all!*

Suddenly, there was a loud knock on the door, and Sir Rufus let himself into the room without being invited.

"Aaah, gentlemen," he said smoothly, "so sorry to interrupt you."

He walked over and settled into a chair next to Diego.

"We were talking about young girls," Kitt said to Rufus. "Mr Diego here is looking for a young 'un."

"Easy enough to arrange," boasted Sir Rufus.

"How is that?" asked Diego, hoping he was hiding his growing irritation.

"Plenty of children bought and sold here. Some are orphans sold to us by industrialists when they turn out to be lazy workers. Some parents need the money, and if they sell one, it feeds the other mouths back at home. There's a constant stream of them. Just tell us what you are looking for. We always pick the best, the prettiest."

Diego and Eduardo were filled with disgust. They were family men who loved and nurtured their children. These two monsters were the antithesis of everything that they stood for. They used all their might to keep up the pretence.

"No, Sir, you do not understand me. I am looking for a particular child. She was in the Guide to Manchester Nightlife. One of your newer recruits, judging by the description. It said she's still a maiden."

Kitt and Sir Rufus eyeballed each other. They only had one chaste girl on their books—Ruby. Rufus who hadn't had his way with her yet scowled at O'Conner.

"We saw an enticing photo in Sneed's guide touting the virginity of a young woman in your establishment. It's her we want."

"Oh yes," answered Rufus, "so sorry old chap, that one has already been bought and paid for. We get a bit creative with the descriptions. Little white lies and all that. We train the girls to act innocent, so it looks like her first time. Keeps the punters happy."

Eduardo put his hand gently on Diego's arm. "Keep calm," he whispered to Diego in Spanish, as Kitt and Rufus fixed themselves a cognac.

"Who bought her?" asked Diego, his eyes narrowing.

"I did," answered Sir Rufus.

Sensing trouble, Eduardo gripped Diego's arm firmly.

"How much did you pay?" asked Eduardo. He didn't trust Diego to speak.

"One hundred pounds," said Kitt.

Sir Rufus sat quietly and crossed his legs at the ankle. He blew a brace of concentric cigar smoke rings into the tense air. It was a most arrogant pose, designed to deliberately annoy Diego and Eduardo.

"I'll give you five hundred pounds—to have her tonight, Mr O'Connor." offered Eduardo coolly.

"What do you mean?" asked Kitt aghast.

"I said I'll raise the bid from one hundred to five hundred pounds," said Eduardo, flicking the thick stack of notes in his hand again.

"Kitt," said Sir Rufus, "you cannot possibly take the offer seriously, after all, we have an agreement, I have given you a down payment, and I brought the girl to you a year ago. Surely that means I get to take her first?"

Eduardo thumped the wad of notes on his hand, desperate for Kitt to bite the bait on the hook. *Come on, man! Diego is going to explode any second.*

"This can't happen, Kitt. We have a deal!" yelled a furious Sir Rufus. "Who is this upstart anyway?"

Diego decided to play his trump card and with two short sentences overturned Rufus's apple cart.

"I am Diego Alaniz, and I am the girl's father. And with a payment of five hundred pounds, she will be mine!"

Eduardo threw the money at Kitt, and it fluttered in the air. They knew his greed would distract him. Sir Rufus stood up to block Diego's path, but the colossal Spaniard flung him aside like a corn dolly. He landed awkwardly banging his head on the corner of a low table and was out for the count.

"¡Rápido, vamos!" yelled Eduardo, and the two friends ran for the study door and flung it open.

Tilly had been waiting outside Kitt's study, wondering why Sir Rufus was late for his usual Friday session. She had heard the argument in full and knew this was the moment to secure Ruby's freedom.

43

THE CAPTIVE IN THE CUPBOARD

"Follow me, Sir!" said Tilly to Diego, grabbing him by the arm. "I'll take you to where we've kept Ruby safe!"

It was time. Kitt was too busy counting the money, and Sir Rufus was barely conscious on the floor.

Tilly showed Eduardo and Diego to the kitchen, and they stormed in, causing quite a stir amongst the staff. Everybody stopped what they were doing and stared at the strange newcomers.

"Where is Ruby? I am her father. Where is she?" he demanded in his thick Spanish accent.

They all looked at each other, nobody wanted to answer.

"It's alright", reassured Tilly. "This is Diego Alaniz. 'E's looked for 'er all over the Meadow. Jimmy's been 'elping 'im. Sneed's rag was running an advert for 'er. That's 'ow 'e traced her 'ere. 'E's paid Sir Rufus's bill and more. She's free to go. Quickly now!"

As she spoke, everybody stepped a little closer to inspect the man. Over the past year, they had become very protective of their precious girl.

"Is she in the cupboard, Cook?" asked Tilly.

"Aye, she is."

"She is where?" asked Diego, puzzled.

"In the cupboard, Sir," said Cook. "We kept her there to protect her from the patrons."

"¡Dios mio! My daughter has had to live in a cupboard for a year to stop being mauled by O'Conner's monsters?" said the murderously angry father.

As Diego ranted, the red mist descended, blinding him with rage. Tilly went to speak to a timid and bewildered Ruby, still in her hiding place, eavesdropping on every word.

"Who is he?"

On hearing a child's voice, Diego fell silent.

"It's your father, Ruby. Diego Alaniz," replied Tilly.

"I don't have a father. He left my mother before she had us. He wrote for a bit, but then he died at sea."

Diego's heart broke.

"Let me speak to her."

He knelt by the hatch and used the soothing voice that always calmed her sister.

"Ruby, dearest—"

She didn't answer him.

"Ruby. You don't have to be afraid."

"Why should I believe that?" asked a soft voice from behind the hatch.

"Because I was married to your mother Grace, after meeting her in the tea shop on Angel Street. Your twin sister Bianca, with blue eyes and ash blonde hair, wants you to come home. You used to live in Angel Meadow, sharing a bed, and you've not seen her since you were four years old. She has a doll she named after you, and that's how I learned about your existence. Your Aunt Agnes was a cruel woman who never told me about you.

I promise that is the only reason we were separated."

She had always remembered Agnes had sent her out on an errand the day she vanished with Bianca, and people said she had got into a posh cab. The wealthy-looking man's story made sense.

Inside the gloomy cupboard, Diego saw a girl peering at him. From the size of her, he deduced she was the same age as Bianca. Her clothes were old and patched, and from her chilblains on her hands, he could see that she had done hard physical labour. His eyes travelled to her face. She had chestnut hair and the darkest eyes he had ever seen, apart from his own.

For one of the few times in her life, Ruby found that panic started to take over. It was all too much to take in. She fought her way out of the cupboard and ran into Cook's arms. Eduardo looked at the child. Her eyes had the same fire in them as her father.

"You don't have to be afraid, lass," said Cook soothingly. "This is your Pa. He's come to rescue you from Sir Rufus and Kitt."

Ruby was terrified, and she wouldn't let go. Her nerves were already in tatters after the strain of her impending night with Sir Rufus, the man who murdered Ida Townsend on a whim, and now this?

Gaining Ruby's trust was proving challenging. Nevertheless, Diego persevered.

"Jimmy Townsend is waiting for us outside. I believe he has been a guardian angel to you since your time in hospital?"

Ruby's eyes brightened. *Jimmy is a good judge of character.* It was Gerhard the German who finally tipped the balance in her mind.

"Come, Ruby," he said, "I vill valk out with you, and I'll make sure that you're safe."

He offered her his hand.

"Can I take Cook with me?" asked Ruby, in tears as once more, the people who cared for her were about to leave her life.

"No, lass," answered Cook with compassion. "I am far too old to go with you. But you can write to me." She smiled, fighting back the tears herself.

Ruby collected a small bag of clothes and left the kitchen, escorted out the back by Gerhard. Kitt's henchmen had abandoned their post at the back garden, off to investigate the tip-off that intruders had assaulted Sir Rufus.

Jimmy was standing around the next corner, waiting for them.

"The carriage is waiting on the wharf, down at the Irk. Come on, let's go! Juan is there already."

The four men and the girl ran down the hill in the dead of night, heels slipping on the grimy cobbles and the stink of the river rising ever more as they got closer to it.

Back at the brothel, Sir Rufus had come back to his senses after the blow to his head. He was so enraged that he was in no fit state to make a good decision. He had no angel on his shoulder that warned him when things had gone too far and that he had lost the fight.

He flung open the back gate, ran down the steps and pursued the shadows down the hill to the wharf. With uncharacteristic agility, thanks to his new-found fight-or-flight fitness, he ran along the waterfront towards Ruby.

Nobody was expecting the attack. He ran up behind Ruby and grabbed her by the hair. She yelped in pain. Drunk and irate, his evil face radiated pure hatred. He gave a stark warning:

"If I can't have her, no one will."

Sir Rufus pulled her towards the water. Ruby twisted and turned but couldn't slip out of his grasp.

It would be Gerhard who ran forward and tackled him. In the mad scramble, Ruby went flying, landing on the hard ground. Ever the independent one, she was on her feet in an instant. All the men were now chasing Sir Rufus. He reached the far end of the waterfront and with misplaced confidence, jumped a ten-foot gap to a wooden gangway. Instead of landing on the walkway, he slipped and fell into the sludgy black water.

"Help me! Help me. I can't swim."

Begging in terror, his bulging, fat, fish-like eyes, stared at them. No one came to his aid. For abusing his ma, Jimmy detested him. Ruby hated him for kidnapping her. Diego and Eduardo reviled him for taking his pleasure with innocent children. They all watched him sink into oblivion, his glassy eyes wide open and his slit of a mouth gasping for air that didn't exist. He would never terrorise anybody again. The evil man was gone.

Diego ran to Ruby and threw his coat around her to keep her warm, keen to leave Manchester as soon as he could.

"How can I thank you?" he said to Gerhard. "You saved my daughter's life."

"I need to leave England, Sir," said Gerhard.

Diego nodded at Eduardo as he climbed into the cab.

"There will be another of my spice ships in the harbour in a fortnight. If you wish to come to Spain, you are welcome. We will assist you." said Eduardo.

"Thank you, Sir," said the German. "May I be so bold as to ask to bring Tilly as vell."

"I'll give the Captain of the vessel instructions to give you both passage. We will arrange for lodgings on your arrival."

They left him, staring thoughtfully at the spot where Sir Rufus had vanished.

Jimmy looked at Ruby as she took her place in the carriage. His mind rushed back to the day when he made friends with her at the hospital. She had been such a serious, fierce little thing. From the moment he had seen her, he had the strong instinct to protect her. He wanted her to be safe and happy.

"Ruby, you are going to be looked after now. You will never be afraid again."

"I don't want to leave you behind, Jimmy. I've known you all my life, I want you to come with me."

Diego nodded at Eduardo again.

"Do you want to learn to sail ships, Jimmy?" offered Eduardo.

"You mean to live on the high seas, not try to sell stale bread in the Meadow? Just let me think about that for a second. Er—yes!" replied Jimmy.

"Well then get in the carriage, Amigo! You are coming to Barcelona with us," said Diego warmly.

Jimmy Townsend looked fit to burst with excitement as he grabbed the carriage's handrail and sprung onto the step!

44

THE DISAPPEARANCE
OF SIR RUFUS

Soon, Sir Rufus's absence would be under investigation. The situation was critical. Diego and Eduardo's buccaneering past was far behind them, and they did not relish the prospect of never being able to sail to England again. It was an important trade centre for them.

Expecting to leave in a hurry with Ruby, the Spaniards had already checked out of the hotel and put their belongings in their trunks. They were confident no one would admit to being at the brothel that night, and any witnesses would crawl back under their stones. They fled at breakneck pace to Liverpool and prepared to set sail.

It was almost first light as they left. Once out of the chaos of the docks, out in the Irish Sea, there was no wind, and the water still and mirror-like. The black and white steamship thudded and rumbled its way back to Barcelona.

Ruby had only ever seen the small barges on the stinking, polluted waters of the River Irk beneath the black Manchester skies. The contrast out at sea was a joy. She breathed the clean sea air deep into her lungs. She smelt the saltwater. She heard gulls cry in the skies. But what impressed her the most was the space, vast amounts of space as far as the eye could see. Where the heavens met the earth at the faraway horizon, there was no line differentiating the two. The peaceful orangey glow of dawn fused into one relaxing expanse.

Ruby and Diego stood on the bridge.

"Can I call you, Captain?" asked Ruby seriously. "I've read about Captain Cook, Magellan, Columbus. They seem very special people."

"If that is what you are comfortable with, yes." smiled Diego.

"I never thought I would ever be on a ship as big as this. Did Brunel design it?" said Ruby.

Her father looked surprised at the breadth of her knowledge.

"I've had plenty of time to read on my own." she grinned.

Ruby had found her voice at last, and there was no stopping her. She was like Grace, delighting in everything. Every morsel of life was a little parcel of joy, and she loved to share her thoughts.

"Can you read and write?" asked Diego.

"Yes. A kind lady called Tess taught me," answered Ruby fondly.

"I promise you, Ruby, that if you learn very hard, one day when you are grown up, I'll teach you to sail this ship."

"Like Juan sails it?" She smiled seriously.

"Yes, like Juan."

Ruby looked at Diego. It was too much for her to grasp. There was so much hardship to forget about in her old life and so many thrilling new avenues to enjoy. *I'm sure I'll never quite experience this freedom again as I sail away from the slums of Manchester.* She had her father's blood in her, the yearning for space and freedom. Whether that was inherited or a consequence of hiding, living cramped up behind curtains and cupboard doors for most of her life, she would always feel gloriously at home out at sea.

As the steamer ploughed its way back to Spain, Diego spent hours watching his beautiful child and thanked the Lord that he had arrived in Angel Meadow—just in time.

45

BACK AT PORT VELL

Being out at sea, Diego had no way to know about an article published in the Manchester Times which reported that Sir Rufus Spencer had been found in a low-class brothel in Angel Meadow near the wharf. He was believed to have suffered heart failure in the bed of a prostitute, Miss Tilly Williams. His doctor, Dr Leighton, who signed the death certificate, said he had been suffering from heart disease for several years. If Diego had seen Kathleen, she would have told him that the word on the street was that Sir Rufus had finally got his comeuppance.

Gerhard the German confessed to Diego that it was he who had retrieved the odious politician from the murky water as soon as the cab left. Gerhard had witnessed enough abuse through the years that carrying Sir Rufus's body up the hill disguised as sacks of coal in a wheelbarrow was easy. The body was scrubbed clean in the kitchen. His wet clothes were not a problem, he was discovered naked in the bed.

The shame and scandal escalated into the highest ranks of government as more parliamentarians were exposed for the same crime. The social upheaval led to investigations in child rape and child prostitution, but Ruby didn't need to know the sordid details that emerged in the wake of her rescue. All that mattered was that she was with her father.

Diego and Ruby sat on the deck together, having tea. He couldn't get the child out of the fresh air, the stiff breeze on deck didn't seem to bother her one bit.

Keen to warm her up, he took her to the bridge, and just like Bianca, she was obsessed with all the dials and levers, curious to know what each one did.

Eduardo smiled.

> "Diego, I think that you have found the person who is going to sail your ships for you, young Ruby there."

> "Why do you say that?"

> "Because I see the same look in her eyes that I saw in yours the day we first went to sea."

Diego laughed long and hard. It was a good sound and the first time Eduardo had heard it in weeks.

The weather was warmer as they approached the Mediterranean. It was a sheer paradise for the girl used to the horrors of the slum. If leaving Liverpool had been liberating, this leg was genuinely magical. Sailing through the Straits of Gibraltar was a memory that would remain with Ruby forever.

On the last day of the sailing, the long-lost twin could think of nothing else but seeing her darling Bianca once more—and the new family that waited for her. Diego, Eduardo and Juan were a delight, and she hoped the people they spoke about would be as lovely as they were. It helped make it seem less daunting.

As the ship docked, a small crowd was gathered on the jetty.

Ruby was dressed in a white dress and red coat that Diego had found in one of the boxes of cargo. It didn't fit very well, but it was good enough for the moment. Her chestnut hair was plaited and hung down her back, almost reaching her waist.

Diego stood at the rail waiting to disembark. He could see everybody waiting for them. Bianca stood at the front, and when the gangway was dropped, she charged up ahead of everybody else. She first rushed into the arms of her Papi. *Oh, I have missed him!*

Remembering her manners, Bianca loosened her grip and turned to face Ruby. There was an awkward moment between the sisters. The onlookers on shore looked on with trepidation. Ruby looked at Bianca, the big blue eyes, the beautiful smile and that joy that was contagious, shone through. After all this time, it really was her.

Then they gave each other a huge hug, to begin to make up for all the smaller ones they must have missed in the years apart.

Carmen's heart overflowed with joy at the sight of their first encounter in years.

"We are going to sleep in the same room. Carmen and I got it ready while Papi was away. It has the biggest bed in it, and we can share it just like when we were small."

Diego smiled. They were friends again. The three of them walked down the gangway hand in hand. Carmen rushed up and took Ruby and Bianca to meet the others, hoping Diego would speak to Maria.

He was ready to speak to her now he was no longer afraid. It was as though he had always known that there was still a part of Grace in Manchester, and he had to go back and find it before he could pursue a new life. He would never forget Grace. He would see her in his daughters every day, but now he was free to love again.

"Hello, Maria."

"I missed you," she said, raising a hand to touch his face.

"Me too!" he said, gazing into her eyes.

"Maria, do you think you could take on an older gentleman with two children."

"It all depends if he loves me." She was serious.

"Of course, he loves you," smiled Diego, "He doesn't want to live without you."

"Then I can take him on," she smiled.

"And you will not run back to Agnes when my back is turned?"

"Oh, I doubt that," said Eduardo quickly. "Selfish to the last, she's stayed in Manchester."

To prove Diego's heart belonged to Maria, he slowly lowered his head and gave her a lingering kiss, pulling her close to his body. Carmen nudged her husband in the ribs.

"Look at that Eduardo! I told you so! ¡Mama mia! I told you they were in love. Let the woman breathe, Diego!"

Carmen laughed with ecstasy. Eduardo sighed and shook his head. The rowdy little crowd walked down the quayside to where the carriages were waiting for them. Porters and yeomen were busy on the wharf as the cargo was offloaded onto carts.

Others at the port stopped to watch the landing party pass by. Diego was holding Ruby's one hand, and Bianca was holding her other.

"Who is that girl with the Captain?" shouted someone in the crowd.

Eduardo tipped his hat to the man and smiled.

"That's one of Diego's greatest treasures, his long-lost Ruby."

Printed in Great Britain
by Amazon

28193822R00187